# A Spot at Starlight Beach

ANJ

Press

Pittsburgh

A SPOT AT STARLIGHT BEACH

ANJ Press, First edition. December 2024

Copyright © 2024 Amelia Addler.

Written by Amelia Addler.

Cover design by Lori Jackson

https://www.lorijacksondesign.com/

Maps by MistyBeee

*for my husband –*
*you make everything possible*

# Recap and Introduction to
# A Spot at Starlight Beach

The third installment of The Spotted Cottage series...

Our story began when divorcée Sheila Dennet moved to San Juan Island, Washington to help her ex-mother-in-law Patty save her beloved tea shop.

Sheila turned everything around – the tea shop, her love life, and even the sad history of an orca whale named Lottie whom her father had accidentally captured forty years ago. With actor boyfriend Russell Westwood's help, she comes up with a plan to retire Lottie from her life of performing.

When Sheila's daughter Eliza moved to the island, she hoped for a quiet refuge. Instead, a bank robbery thrust her into the spotlight and put her on the trail of a wanted criminal. With the help of Joey, Russell's seaplane pilot, she was able to catch the bank robber, clear her good name, and find new love.

Now Sheila's eldest daughter Mackenzie has made the move to the island. After discovering her boyfriend had another girlfriend (now fiancée), Mackenzie wants nothing to do with romance.

Unfortunately for her, the island has other plans...

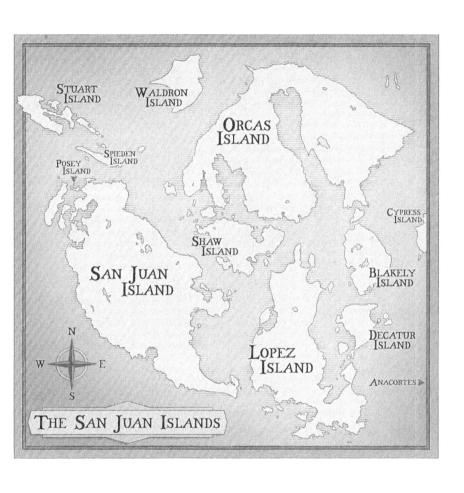

# One

The first time Mackenzie cared about Shakespeare was in high school English when her rival, the class valedictorian, recited a verse from *As You Like It*:

*All the world's a stage,*
*And all the men and women merely players...*

The delivery was horrendous, but with the first two lines, Mackenzie knew what the ancient poet was going on about. Life was a game – one she could win.

Just as her teacher had insisted, the themes were as timeless as human nature. Mackenzie wrote a paper likening Shakespeare's disguised Rosalind to Robin William's Mrs. Doubtfire, earning a perfect grade in the class.

It was so easy that she saw no need to read old Bill again – until a decade later when she burst into tears watching a video of Andrew Scott performing *To be or not to be*.

How had it taken her ten years to really *hear* Shakespeare? Yes, she'd heard the words as a schoolgirl, but they didn't hit her square in the chest like this until she was twenty-seven, sitting on a bunk bed in her granny's cottage, single, unemployed, and sucked into a cruel internet algorithm forcing her to watch an endless stream of videos into the wee morning hours.

That was what it took for her to listen. She needed a breakdown to let it in.

Granted, the breakdown came relatively quickly. She'd only officially been out of work for two weeks, but time had lost all meaning because there was so much pressure on her.

She was supposed to be finding her next career, or finding herself, whatever that meant. She was supposed to look like a delusional woman in a drug commercial, smiling at the sun, not like a ghostly shadow floating in front of a screen.

Was this what happened to people when they retired? They finally got freedom only to find their lives empty, only to discover work was never the problem?

Maybe Mackenzie had been the problem all along. Or maybe too much freedom wasn't a good thing. Or, heaven forbid, maybe she was getting soft.

There was no way to be sure, but she needed answers. The next morning, she woke early, washed her hair, and got to the library as soon as it opened.

The first section that pulled her in was the self-help books. Only the most absurd titles caught her eye: *Sparkle and Shine, How to Reclaim your Inner Diva,* and worst of all, *Seven Steps to Unleash Your Unique Unicorn.*

None of these would do. She walked on, past the children stacking blocks, past the man hunched over the keyboard looking over his shoulder, until she found a brown, linen hardcover copy of *As You Like It.*

Next to a dinosaur statue, sitting in a chair shaped like an open hand, she read past the famous first lines.

*All the world's a stage,*
*And all the men and women merely players;*
*They have their exits and their entrances;*
*And one man in his time plays many parts,*
*His acts being seven ages.*

Seven ages. How had she not caught that before? What age was she in? She read on:

*At first the infant,*
*Mewling and puking in the nurse's arms;*

She was past that. Probably.

*And then the whining school-boy, with his satchel*
*And shining morning face, creeping like snail*
*Unwillingly to school.*

Nope. Way past that.

*And then the lover,*
*Sighing like furnace, with a woeful ballad*
*Made to his mistress' eyebrow...*

Her dalliance with her ex-boss fit there. It was the entire reason she had to hastily leave her job and flee to San Juan Island. That part of her life was *definitely* over. What came next?

*Then a soldier,*
*Full of strange oaths, and bearded like the pard...*

Soldier? Mackenzie didn't feel like a soldier, and certainly not a bearded one. She had two chin hairs, yes, but she stayed on top of them.

*Jealous in honour, sudden and quick in quarrel,*
*Seeking the bubble reputation*
*Even in the cannon's mouth...*

Mackenzie slapped the book shut and stood, knocking the hand chair to the floor. She righted it, then returned the book to its spot, her face stinging red.

How had Shakespeare managed to call her out like that? Hadn't he been dead for hundreds of years? Had he even been a real person?

She dodged the librarian's eye and scooted out the door. It was as though Shakespeare himself had traveled through the centuries to tease her for chasing that woman through town last week when she hadn't picked up her dog's business.

But her mom wasn't going to say anything about it, and the lady deserved to be publicly shamed! Mackenzie couldn't help it if she was better with confrontation than most people!

And she would never stick her head "in the cannon's mouth." That wasn't her style.

Unless, of course, the cannon came to her.

• • •

The next morning, Russell showed up at the tea shop with a bag of bagels from the mainland.

"Hey, Mackenzie," he said. "Can we talk?"

The white paper bag crinkled as she peeked inside – cinnamon raisin, asiago, marble rye. There was a tub of cream cheese pushed to the side, a thin wooden knife sticking straight up.

Mackenzie hadn't had a bagel since she'd gotten to the island. Maybe that was the source of her madness?

She pulled out the cinnamon raisin and split it in half, spreading the white fluff a finger thick. "What's up, Russ?"

He sat across from her. "You know I had to fire my assistant."

In fact, there were two tubs of cream cheese, one plain and one cinnamon-flavored. She'd grabbed the cinnamon, the heavy spice drifting up to her nostrils. What a delight.

She looked up. "So it was your assistant stealing money after all?"

He nodded. "The police confirmed it today."

Mackenzie had only met the assistant once. She was supposed to manage all the details related to the rehabilitation and relocation of Lottie the whale.

Problems arose almost as soon as she'd started working there. It was easy to blame it on growing pains, and the assistant even went on the news to decry someone stealing from the poor animal's fund.

Mackenzie chewed through a big bite of bagel. "That stinks."

"Yeah. It's bad." He leaned closer. "At least a hundred thousand stolen from our fundraising account, plus I found out she never paid a bunch of invoices for supplies."

A hunk of bagel caught in her throat. She coughed, rushing to take a sip of water. "Can you get it back?"

"I think so." A smile spread across his face. "If you'll help me."

She set down her water. "Oh, no. No, no, no. I'm not getting involved in that mess. No thank you."

"Hear me out."

Her eyes watered. The bagel hunk would forever be embedded in her throat.

She blinked at him.

He went on. "I'm leaving to shoot *Fangs of Waterloo* tomorrow, and I need someone here I can trust."

Mackenzie snorted on her water. *Fangs of Waterloo.* It would never not be funny to her that Russell's fans voted to have him star in a historical vampire romance. Merciless. Hilarious. He was only doing it to raise money for Lottie, which made it even funnier. "Then hire someone trustworthy."

He smiled, tilting his head down at her. "I'm trying to, but she's eating all of my bagels and refusing to listen to what I'm saying."

Mackenzie laughed, covering her mouth with her hand. "Guilty as charged."

"You would just need to watch over things. Be a point of contact. Act as my eyes on the ground. It won't be for long. The movie shoots for eleven weeks and, after that, I'll be back. I'll hire someone new."

She raised an eyebrow. "You won't be back in time for the Blackfish Ball?"

"No, but it's *mostly* planned, and—"

"I'm not an event planner, Russell. And I know nothing about building a retirement sea pen for a killer whale."

"Margie will take care of the details for the ball, and you don't need to know anything else. Just pay invoices, keep up on timelines, make sure the contractors show up. Don't steal from Lottie." He sighed. "*Please*, Mackenzie? I'll pay you well, and it'll be the easiest job you've ever had."

Mackenzie eyed him. She was in need of a job, but this? This sounded like a nightmare. "That's too bad, because I don't like easy jobs. I like a challenge."

"By all means, challenge yourself! Take charge of the fundraising. Make the Blackfish Ball an event to remember. I'm betting you could replace all the money that was stolen."

"Or double it."

She paused. Was that her soldier era speaking, or was that just her?

"That's the spirit." He grinned and sat back.

She dusted her hands off with a napkin. "There has to be someone else you can go to. I'm a saleswoman, Russell. I wouldn't know where to start with this."

He frowned. "I leave in less than twelve hours. I don't trust anyone else."

"Maybe you shouldn't trust me." She leaned forward, eyes wide. "Do you know I spent three hours yesterday researching hotels in London? I've never been to London. I'll probably never get to go, or get to see the Globe Theatre."

"Sounds like you need to focus on something productive."

Mackenzie scowled. "Yeah, but not this."

"I'll find someone else to take over when I get back. But right now, Lottie needs help. I'll be running around Brussels dressed as a vampire, and I don't have anyone to keep things running smoothly here. Lottie might not make it to her sea pen without you. She needs you, Mackenzie."

She pursed her lips. The image of Lottie floating aimlessly in that little tank flashed through her mind. The poor thing didn't even have videos to watch. Just a blank wall to stare at under the hot sun.

*Actors.* They knew how to twist the knife. "Fine. I'll do it. But for Lottie, and no one else."

"Hey!" he shouted, clapping his hands together. "I knew you'd come to your senses!"

Russell left for Belgium that evening, taking Sheila with him. Eliza was busy canoodling with her new boyfriend Joey, Granny was already snoring, and Mackenzie was left to sit in her bunk, sorting through the documents the old assistant had left behind.

Shakespeare had no idea what he was talking about. She wasn't a soldier trying to prove herself. She was a woman making a boring spreadsheet about overdue invoices. A woman resisting the urge to look at her cheating ex-boyfriend's Instagram. A woman who let herself look just *once* after she finished scouring the Excel sheet.

She wasn't a soldier. This wasn't a battle. It would all be fine, she told herself as she fell asleep.

And it was fine. For the first twelve hours.

# Two

The tea shop was their moment of refuge. Dark wood, heavy chairs, and little silver bells on the tables. The air was warm, but not too warm, and smelled of cinnamon.

Cameron peeked through the window. A minivan sat in the parking lot, lights on and engine humming.

"I can't believe they were so blatant about following us here." Cameron tried to pull the curtains closed over the windows, but they refused to budge. "Does this happen to you all the time?"

Bailey Jo shrugged. "It depends. It's gotten worse since I did the Super Bowl. People recognize me everywhere now. I'm sure it'll die down eventually..."

"Amazing performance, by the way." Cameron put a hand to his chest. "I was blown away."

She smiled. "Thank you."

A wrinkled lady strode out of a swinging door. Her cheeks were rosy red, and she had spectacles perched on the edge of her nose.

"Here for some tea?" she asked.

Bailey Jo stepped forward. "I *love* your apron!"

The woman looked down at the pink-and-white striped smock. "Thank you! Made it myself."

"It's lovely. My grandma used to make us aprons like that."

A second woman, this one much younger, walked out from the swinging door and stopped dead when she saw Bailey Jo.

"You can sit wherever you like," the older woman said. "I'll get some menus."

"We're actually not here for tea," Cameron said, stepping forward. "I was hoping to catch Russell."

"I'm afraid Russell isn't stateside." She nodded to a chalkboard with a hand-drawn pot of tea and a list of flavors. "We've got an orange chai this month you won't want to miss."

"Granny..." The younger woman cleared her throat, her voice barely above a whisper. "That's Bailey Jo Collins."

Granny looked back, smiling. "Is she a friend of yours?"

"No," she stammered, "she's a *brilliant* singer and—"

The front door opened and four women burst in. They stood in a gaggle, whispering.

This was only going to keep escalating. Cameron sighed. "May we go somewhere more private?"

The younger woman nodded eagerly. "This way."

She led them through a glass door and onto a patio overlooking the sea. Black wrought iron tables stood against the wind as light danced on the water in the distance.

"Sorry about that." Cameron offered a handshake. "I think some fans followed us from Friday Harbor. I'm Cameron Walters."

"Eliza Dennet," she said with a smile, turning away from him and toward Bailey Jo. "It's so nice to meet you, Bailey Jo. I'm a huge fan, I think you're awesome, and I love your music."

"That's so kind," Bailey Jo said, extending a handshake. "It's nice to meet you, too. I love your tea shop!"

Granny appeared, slamming the glass door behind her, a plate stacked with speckled scones in her hand. "Don't be shy —take a seat. Eliza just pulled these from the oven."

Bailey Jo walked to a table, following the sweet-faced grandma like a baby duck after its mother.

Cameron tapped Eliza on the shoulder.

She stayed behind, but her eyes lingered on Bailey Jo. "Can I help you?"

"I didn't mean to drop in on you like this," he said in a low voice. "I work for a travel company called Opuluxe Escapes. Bailey Jo came to me as a potential client, and I'm trying to close my sale."

"Oh?" Her eyes darted to the table where Bailey Jo and her new grandma were huddled over the plate of scones.

Cameron went on. "Bailey Jo is a wildlife enthusiast – eagles, bears, whales. All that jazz. I'm trying to charter a polar cruise for her, and I wanted to check if the sea pen site would be useful for one of the stops. She heard about that whale you have up there and she's *very* intrigued."

"You mean Lottie?" Eliza asked with a frown. "We don't have her here. Not yet."

He waved a hand. "I'm sure there are other whales. Anyway, Bailey Jo wanted to make sure she'd be welcome, and that it wouldn't be too difficult for her mom to get around. She walks with a cane and – it doesn't matter. I emailed Russell Westwood a few weeks ago. He said we could stop by."

Eliza sucked in a breath. "Russell. Right. Uh, he's not here right now."

A face in the window caught his eye – a woman's forehead drawn tight, her lips pursed into a scowl. She mouthed something at Eliza, who shook her head vigorously in return.

The door to the patio flew open and the woman emerged. "Why is there a group of rowdy women in the lobby?"

"Mackenzie, this is Cameron," Eliza said. She jerked her head to the side. "He's working for Bailey Jo Collins!"

Mackenzie peered over her shoulder. "Okay."

There were far too many people to deal with at this place. How many employees did one tea shop need? And where was Russell?

"Hey there, Mackenzie. It's nice to meet you," Cameron said, forcing a smile. "I was just telling Eliza that I talked to Russell a few weeks ago. He was open to the sea pen becoming a stop on our luxury polar cruise."

"Uh huh." She crossed her arms over her chest. "Russell isn't around, so you'll have to check back in a few weeks."

Cameron blinked at her, the smile frozen on his face. "I was told there's a pilot who can take us out there for a look? Maybe I'll talk to him."

"Not right now, no." She shook her head.

"Mackenzie..." Eliza hissed. "This is *Bailey Jo*."

"What are you girls whispering about?" Granny yelled. "Don't be rude. Come over here! Talk to Bailey! And grab a scone while they're hot!"

Eliza spun, taking off toward the table. Cameron managed to grab Mackenzie's elbow.

She turned and glared at him, her lips twisted.

"I don't expect you to get it," he said quietly. "You're not interested in what I'm selling, but I have to try. I'm a salesman. Bailey Jo is my biggest client, and I have to put together a special experience."

Mackenzie pulled her arm away. "I'm a saleswoman myself, so I *do* get it."

He tilted his head to the side. "Are you? What do you sell?"

"Software." She shrugged. "I'm taking a break from it right now."

"Interesting. I've heard selling tech is one of the easiest things to make a living in." He locked eyes with her. "Sells itself, almost."

Her eyes narrowed ever so slightly. "Does it? Because I'd think selling overpriced cruises to the rich and famous might be a bit easier."

A gust of wind blew through his hair, drying the sweat on his forehead. He smiled. "That almost sounds like a challenge."

Mackenzie crossed her arms over her chest. "You know, it does."

She walked past him and took a seat at the table. "Hi, I'm Mackenzie Dennet. I'm in charge of the sea pen operations until Russell gets back. Would you like some tea?"

"No, thank you. I don't mean to be a bother," Bailey Jo said.

Cameron stood behind Bailey Jo, blocking the peering eyes from the tea shop.

"It's no bother at all. It's what we do here." Mackenzie flashed her white teeth. "Cameron tells me you're an animal lover?"

"I am! I'm hoping to take a polar cruise this year. It's on my mom's bucket list – just something really special we can do together."

"There's one place you won't be seeing me," Granny said with a laugh. "The North Pole! Too cold!"

Cameron bit his lip. There was a Mrs. Claus joke in there, but he wasn't going to try it.

"How did you hear about Lottie?" Mackenzie asked.

"Friends, mostly," Bailey Jo said. "I'm fascinated with what Russell is doing. Inspired, really. Has he gotten her out of that amusement park yet?"

"Not yet. She's supposed to be transported in a few weeks." Mackenzie sat back. "We have a team of researchers and veterinarians planning her return. The idea is to retire her, in a way. Keep her safe in the sea pen while increasing her quality of life. I'm sure they'd love to talk to you."

Cameron glanced down. Bailey Jo was beaming. Eating this up.

Unbelievable.

"I always wanted to be a marine biologist," Bailey Jo said. "I think that's what I would've done if my music hadn't taken off. Sometimes I feel like I should still go back to school. Do something that matters."

"But you *do* do something that matters. I *love* your music!" Eliza said breathlessly. "You bring so much joy to peoples' lives."

"Can't downplay the importance of that," Granny said. "Even if you can't always see it for yourself."

"Thank you." Bailey Jo smiled. "That means a lot."

Cameron could feel a glare boring into him. He looked up. It was Mackenzie, giving him the side eye.

She was smiling too.

He clenched his jaw. Why did it feel like he was getting outplayed here? Why wasn't she fawning over Bailey Jo like a normal person?

Mackenzie leaned in. "You know, the researchers do a trip up to the arctic every year. Or at least, they try to – if they have the funding."

"That is so neat!"

"You could go with them. Be part of the research. It'd really be a once-in-a-lifetime experience. I'm sure they'd roll out the red carpet for you and your mom."

Bailey Jo's eyes widened. "Really? Would they want to do that?"

Cameron cut in. "I'm sure that'd be fun, but the level of comfort on those boats can't compare to a chartered ship."

Mackenzie shrugged. "I bet you could charter any boat you wanted. The researchers might like a little comfort."

"I don't mind roughing it. I grew up on a farm."

"Hey, whatever you prefer." She pulled her phone out of her pocket. "But it would be more unique than some cookie-cutter boat trip."

Cameron held his breath. Surely she was going to ask for a selfie? Show some semblance of normalcy around this megastar?

"I'll text Inge. She's one of the whale researchers we're working with. Maybe they're planning to make a trip after Lottie is settled..."

*She cannot be serious.* Cameron sucked in a breath. Mackenzie was stealing his sale!

"Thanks so much for that, Mackenzie," Cameron said, clearing his throat. "I'll take her number. I'm happy to coordinate everything."

"There's no need," Mackenzie said with a gracious smile. Her phone dinged, and she paused to read a message. "She's at the sea pen site right now. You could pop in and say hello. What do you say?"

"That sounds *amazing*," Bailey Jo said with a grin.

"Great! I can ask our pilot to give you a lift. He should be around here somewhere."

Granny stood. "Let me pack some treats for you and Inge! It's not every day we get a star at the tea shop."

"Unless you count Russell," Eliza said.

"I stopped counting him ages ago," Granny said with a chuckle.

Bailey Jo stood. "Do you mind if I use your restroom before we go?"

Eliza shot to her feet. "I can show you where it is!"

He watched the three of them disappear into the tea shop. Mackenzie sat, focused on her phone, texting away, not a care in the world.

Cameron should have been mad, but he was too intrigued.

"I have to hand it to you," he said. "You stole that sale right out from under me."

"It was for the greater good." Mackenzie stood, dusting off her shoulder with her hand, a smirk on her face. "I mean...you kind of asked for it."

He laughed. "I kind of did ask for it." The only thing worse than a sore loser was a charming winner. "I clearly underestimated the finesse you acquired in tech sales."

"Clearly."

"Are you looking for a new position? In sales?"

She paused. "I am, but not right now. For the next few weeks, I'm helping Russell with this project."

"How about after you're done stealing sales here, you come and work for me?"

She laughed and pulled open the door to the tea shop, waving him in. "Yeah. I'll think about it."

"I'm serious." He followed her inside. "Someone as charming, quick-thinking, and beautiful as yourself won't be on the market for long."

The group of women had doubled in size, their voices bouncing off one another in the lobby, crowding the small space.

"You talk about me like I'm the hottest house on the market," Mackenzie said.

"Not a house, no. Maybe a Porsche." Coincidentally, Cameron had always wanted a Porsche.

The front door opened, forcing two scowling women forward.

A man peeked in, shimmying behind them. He had a bag slung over his shoulder and a pair of black sunglasses covering his eyes.

Cameron's throat tightened. If he didn't know any better, he would swear that was Liam Yorkley.

As if his luck couldn't get any worse.

He ducked his head low, beneath the crowd. "I think I'll sneak Bailey Jo through the back, if that's all right."

"Sure. I'll have Joey, our pilot, meet you outside."

"Consider my offer," Cameron said, pressing his business card into her palm. "Lovely losing a sale to you, Mackenzie."

She smiled. "The pleasure was all mine."

He hated to run just then, but he had no choice. He would be back – and he wasn't going to take no for an answer.

# Three

The tea shop door knocked into Liam's shoulder. He stepped forward, his bag hitting the woman in front of him. She shot a snarling look over her shoulder.

"Pardon me," he muttered, stepping sideways into a wall, rattling the pictures in their frames.

"Is she really here?" a woman whispered behind him.

"She'd better be. I left work for this."

A voice called out, "Bailey Jo, I love you!"

More shouting, more shoving. Liam pressed himself against the wall.

This couldn't be the right place. It was awful here.

A loud whistle rang out and the room fell silent.

"Listen up! If you're here for Bailey Jo, you've just missed her."

It was as though the space deflated, letting out a huge, collective groan.

"Let us see her!"

"We know she's here!"

"If you'd like some tea," the authoritative voice continued, "you're welcome to stay. We have poppy seed muffins and an orange chai latte that'll ease your sorrows. Otherwise, see you next time!"

The group of women who had forced him into the wall filed past him and through the front door. Others followed in pairs and trios. When the floodwaters receded, the room was empty save for Liam and the woman who'd done the yelling.

She was tall, nearly as tall as he was, with short blonde hair that was dark at the roots. She had unsmiling red lips and her gray eyes scanned the room as though looking for bombs.

Liam stiffened his shoulders and took a step toward her. "Hello, I'm Liam Yorkley."

She raised an eyebrow. "Are you here for tea?"

Tea. What a dream it'd be to have a cup of tea. His throat was raw from sleeping with his mouth open on the overnight train to Anchorage. He hadn't managed to catch any sleep on the flight to Seattle, and the seaplane ride into Friday Harbor had been delayed by five hours.

"Thank you, but I'm eager to get settled."

Her brow furrowed. "Settled where?"

The knot in his stomach tightened. He'd meant to get something to eat when he landed but it had seemed like too much hassle.

He took a deep breath. "Is Russell here? He'd told me to have the pilot fly me to Stuart Island. I spoke to Joey, I think it was? He said he needed clearance first."

"Who are you, exactly?"

"Liam Yorkley." His voice rose. "I met Russell in Denali National Park. I was the artist in residence there, and he invited me to stay on Stuart for a few weeks as the artist in residence."

A second woman rounded the corner, a black apron tied around her waist. She smiled when she saw him. "Hi! Can I help you?"

"Unless you can get me to Stuart Island, I doubt it."

"Since when do we have an artist in residence?" the blonde asked.

The other woman gasped. "Oh wait. I think he mentioned this to me."

"But not to me, his assistant?" The blonde rolled her eyes. "I'm going to kill him."

"Great. Do that, then you can take me next." Liam dropped his bag on the floor. "But at least have the decency to give me a cup of tea first."

The blonde narrowed her eyes. "All right, Liam Yorkley, this isn't about you. It's about my mom's boyfriend, Russell. He's not great with details."

Liam let out a breath. "I see that."

"I'm Eliza. It's nice to meet you," the aproned one said. "I'll get you something. Yorkshire tea? We get it from London."

It was sure to be horrible. "Thank you."

"With milk?" she added.

He nodded, rubbing his shoulder. The bag was heavier than he'd realized, perhaps adding to his snappiness. "Please."

"I wasn't aware you were coming," the blonde said, her tone decided much flatter. "I'm Mackenzie. I'm filling in as Russell's assistant."

"Hello, Mackenzie. Liam."

"You mentioned that," she said with a smirk. "Have a seat. Joey should be able to fly you out once you finish your tea."

"Thank you."

He was already embarrassed by what he'd said, though he couldn't remember exactly what it was, only the sentiment, which was pierced with flame.

He walked as far from Mackenzie as possible, slipping into a chair by a window. It was wood, and hardly comfortable, but each second sunk him deeper into it, the muscles in his back and legs relaxing.

How many hours had it taken to get here? He had lost count, but clearly his body had not.

Light streamed through the window, falling onto the pastel linens. Pink and white flowers danced on the wallpaper, and doilies dusted the tables. He stared at them, unable to decide which of the two women who had greeted him had come up with such garish decorations.

However, miraculously, by the time his tea arrived, he almost liked the décor.

"Sorry about the confusion," Eliza said, setting a plate in front of him. "I got you a few treats too – on the house. Welcome to the island!"

He forced a smile, avoiding her eyes. "That's very kind. Thank you."

There was a scone glazed with lines of sugar, a cookie dusted with cinnamon, and a small lemon loaf. She'd supplied a ramekin of butter with a little knife.

Liam picked up the scone and took a bite. Bits of orange and cranberry balanced the sugar, the flavors bursting in his mouth.

The dull ache in his stomach released. He quickly took another bite.

"That is quite good. Thank you," he said.

"I know how hard it is to be far from home."

He glanced up. She was looking down at him, smiling. There was nothing like kindness to bring the shame of his rudeness into the light.

"I'm sorry for my crabbiness—" he said, but she cut him off.

"Please. I understand. Getting here takes forever and many, many things can go wrong. But you're here now! I think you're going to like it."

Steam rose from his teacup. He tipped in a bit of milk. "You might be right."

"I'm going to get you another tea to try."

"No, that's quite all right."

Too late. She was gone. He took a sip of tea and, outside, the sun peeked out from behind the clouds.

It was, shockingly, quite good.

# Four

The next person Russell "forgot" to mention to her was going to be sent away until tomorrow. Mackenzie had had enough surprises.

She followed Eliza into the kitchen and leaned against the counter. "Is there anyone else I need to fight today?"

Steam rose from the blue and gold teapot as Eliza poured in the hot water. "I'm sure we could find someone."

"Why are you using Granny's nice china? I thought that was for special occasions."

"Liam *is* special, Mack." Eliza set a matching teacup onto a tray. "He's an artist, and he's the first English person I've served in the English tearoom."

Mackenzie groaned. "Here we go."

"What?" She put her hands on her hips. "Maybe he can help us make the experience more genuine. I don't think Granny's been to Britain in forty years."

"He doesn't seem like the helpful type," Mackenzie muttered.

She lifted the tray. "Don't sass at me. The only one you should be angry with is Russell. Why don't you call him and leave him a message about how furious you are? Will that make you feel better?"

Mackenzie didn't appreciate her mockery, but she'd let it slide for now. "He's a terrible communicator. I'm not going to call him. I have it all under control."

"Russell prefers to communicate things on a need-to-know basis," Joey said, popping his head into the kitchen.

Eliza grinned when she saw him. "Hey!"

"From now on, I need to talk to him at least once a week to see what disasters he's left for me," Mackenzie said.

Granny walked in, a container of cookies in her hands. "Where did all the people go?

"They weren't here for us, sadly," Eliza said. "They were here for Bailey Jo."

Granny set the cookies on the counter. "My goodness, what a disappointment!"

"Granny, did you know anything about an artist in residence staying at the sea pen site? A guy named Liam?" Eliza asked.

Granny's face brightened with a smile. "Yes! Apparently Russell found him lying in the grass, waiting for wolves."

"Is that the guy who was looking for a ride today?" Joey asked. "He seemed harmless, but I've learned my lesson. I won't fly anyone without knowing who they are."

"No more bank robbers," Eliza said with a smile.

"I don't care if he is a bank robber. Please get him out of here," Mackenzie said. "I was in the middle of applying to jobs when all this madness broke out."

He saluted. "Aye aye, captain. I've already got Bailey Jo and Cameron in the plane. Is Liam ready to fly out?"

"Who knows?" Mackenzie shrugged at the door. "He's all yours."

"I'll get him on the next flight, actually. One more thing," he said, popping open the lid to the cookies. "I'm going to need one of these."

"Take them all!" Granny said with a sigh. "No one else will appreciate them."

Joey picked up the pale green plastic tub. "Don't mind if I do."

He disappeared, and a moment later, Eliza pulled her head out of a cupboard. "I want Liam to try this one."

"Are you seeking his approval or something?" Mackenzie asked, arms crossed over her chest.

She narrowed her eyes. "I promised him another tea, Mackenzie. Tea is very important to the English. Don't you know anything?"

She clenched her teeth. Were they having a competition to see who could annoy her the most?

Granny reached above her head and pulled down a bronze and black tea tin. "What about this one? I think it's for a more refined palate."

"Refined palate?" Mackenzie scoffed. "I can't with you two."

Eliza accepted the tea with a smile. She set the strainer into the cup, dumped a scoop of the loose leaves, and slowly poured in steaming water.

A bell rang out.

She looked up. "Shoot."

Mackenzie stuck out her hand. "I'll take it to him."

"But be *nice*," Eliza said.

She bulged her eyes out and snatched the mug. "I *am* nice."

She peeked into the English tearoom – his table was empty, the plates neatly stacked.

How rude. Eliza was going through all this trouble and he'd run away?

She dumped the teacup on the table, then weaved past the couple in the lobby and burst through the front door. She stopped. Liam stood just outside the shop, a phone to his ear, his back to her.

"Seems it's all sorted, so don't worry." He ran a hand through his hair. "My last step was getting past the nepotism hire." He laughed. "Yeah. All right."

"I have your tea inside, sir," Mackenzie announced.

He turned, lowering the phone. "Oh, right. Just making a call. Thanks."

Yeah, she'd heard.

"Nepotism hire," she muttered, stepping back inside.

She wasn't a nepotism hire! She hadn't wanted this! She was a nepotism *hostage*!

"Mackenzie!" Granny called out. "Is this yours?"

She held up a white business card – the one Cameron had slipped into her hand before he left.

"Yes, it is. It's from that guy who came in with Bailey Jo."

Granny smiled, tapping it on the register. "Oh, he liked you. I could tell."

"Please, Granny. He's a salesman. The last thing I need in my life is another salesman."

"That's true," Eliza said, appearing at her side.

"Ah!" Mackenzie yelled. "Don't sneak up on me like that!"

"I didn't sneak!" She grinned. "Why'd he give you his card?"

The gold embossed letters of his name flashed light up at her. "He thinks I have a promising future selling luxury trips."

She looked up, blankly staring at Eliza until they both burst into laughter.

"What's so funny? You handled that Bailey Jo very well." said Granny. "Why wouldn't he want to work with you?"

"Or fall in love with you," whispered Eliza.

"Stop it." Mackenzie tucked the card into her pocket. "If his job is selling overpriced trips to rich people, I think I'd make a fortune. But I'm sure there's more to it."

"Don't chase fortunes, dear. Let them come to you," Granny said with a nod.

"Isn't that what he did? Came here to meet Mackenzie?" Eliza asked. "Looking for love, perhaps?"

Mackenzie threw her hands up. "Okay, thank you. I'm done with this conversation. I will see you ladies later."

She spun on her heel and walked directly into Liam's chest.

"Sorry," he said.

She stepped back. "Joey will take you on his next flight. Eliza prepared another tea for you to try. Have a nice day."

Mackenzie went back to her laptop. She'd had enough of Liam. And Eliza was wrong – she wasn't interested in love. She wasn't interested in a quasi-legitimate sales job, either.

Maybe, at the very least, she'd make Cameron split the commission with her on Bailey Jo's cruise. She could use the money, and it was the least he could do.

She slipped the card into her pocket. Best to hold on to it, just in case.

# Five

H is alarm went off before sunrise. Liam woke easily, breathing in the cool, salted air as he walked along the beach, stones shifting beneath him.

In the darkness, it was hard to spot the time-lapse camera he'd left atop the hill. He walked up to check on it, reviewing the comings and goings of ships and birds and lounging seals.

The walk up the hill was familiar to him now, and he rarely stumbled carrying canvases and his bag of paints. He liked to be there as the sun appeared, ready to capture the colors and shadows just as they were.

He set up, paintbrush in hand, and scanned the horizon. Should he focus on the water again?

No. He already had five landscapes like that. Maybe the boat tied up at the dock? It had interesting curves...

Liam dipped his paintbrush and made the first strokes, watching as the sun's rays glimmered off the polished hull.

Five minutes in, he set his paintbrush down. This wasn't right. No one needed this painting. He didn't want it, and no one would want to buy it. Or at least, he didn't think so. He had yet to try his luck at the farmer's market.

He took the canvas and chucked it to the ground. It was just an eight by ten. Nothing special. He was running low on five by sevens. People liked those – they fit into luggage easily. Great to sell to tourists, little mementos of the places they'd been.

He'd keep one of the paintings from this island. Maybe send it to his mom for safekeeping. It was a charming place, despite the difficulty in getting here.

Liam had almost turned down the residency. It made no sense to him – a Hollywood star hiring an artist in residence just because they'd had a pleasant conversation about wolves for an hour or two?

Unheard of.

He set his paintbrush down. Maybe today wasn't a day to paint. His motivation was wavering. He'd initially thought he'd need to sell a few paintings at the farmer's market to get by for the month, but surprisingly, Russell's promise of a stipend came to fruition. That morning, Liam had gotten an email from his bank: **Large deposit credited to your account.**

The sum was generous. Shockingly so. More money than Liam had had in over a year. And Russell really meant to give him that much every month? Maybe it was the sum for the entirety of his residency.

Once he got over the shock of seeing the number, his suspicions started creeping up. Russell clearly wanted something from him. The money had to be a bribe, trying to convince him to make a documentary about the whale – an idea Russell had floated after they'd met.

Liam stood, stretching. Filmmaking wasn't his thing anymore. He'd told that to Russell at the time. Russell seemed to think he was playing hard to get.

"You're telling me you're a filmmaker, yet after two hours of us talking, you still haven't tried to shove one of your scripts down my throat?" Russell had asked him over beers.

"I don't have any scripts," Liam said with a shrug.

"Have you made any films?"

"I used to make short films, yeah." Liam looked up from the menu. "Nothing with wolves, though."

That made Russell laugh. Liam passed along the link to his website – it still held all his old work – and thought nothing of it. The next day, Russell had called to chat about a potential Lottie documentary.

"No pressure, and your residency is unrelated," he'd said, "but you have a keen eye, and I like your style. I think you could put together something amazing about our little Lottie."

Liam thought Russell had to be exceptionally desperate to entertain the idea of hiring a nobody like him to make this documentary. The most Liam would offer was, "I'll think about it."

He made his way down the hill, walking by a builder who nodded a hello. Liam nodded back. The people were friendly here. Cheerful even, if in a gruff sort of way, and always busy.

Maybe Russell was overpaying them, too.

He walked along the buildings dotting the shore. These were picturesque and deserved a closer eye. In truth, there was too much to paint here. It was hard to pick.

Even if he wanted to film a documentary, what was there to tell? The days were all the same. Birds flying overhead. The foreman arriving promptly at eight. Researchers zipping in and out on boats or on Joey's seaplane.

Maybe Russell had asked him because no one else was interested. Or maybe Russell was so difficult to work with that no one with half a brain would take the project. Why else would a Hollywood star need help from someone like him?

Liam spotted a delightfully plump seal lounging on a rock. He grabbed a canvas and set himself up, painting the round belly and shining whiskers.

He'd nearly finished the seal when he heard a rumble of voices. He looked up. The foreman was on the dock, throwing his hands in the air. Liam had never heard him raise his voice, and now he was gesticulating wildly and shouting into his phone.

The seal looked up, lazily casting a glance toward the sound before settling back down.

Something was up. Perhaps this was the sign of the first, and only, drama this island would see.

Fights always amused Liam. Not physical ones – Liam despised violence – but arguments. They were hilarious to witness from the outside – the red faces, the gestures, the spit flying from mouths. Adults behaving like toddlers.

Shouts bounced off the rocks and echoed in his ears. The foreman wasn't out of control by any means, but it could turn into something. Liam stood up and went back to his room, dropping off the seal painting. His video camera was in his suitcase, untouched. It might be worth taking it out, even if he didn't plan to do anything with the footage.

He pulled it out and turned it on, recording as he walked down to the dock.

"Morning, Liam," the foreman said, his boots hitting the wooden dock with heavy strides. His face was flushed, his tone more clipped than usual.

"Morning. Everything all right?"

"Not really." He jerked his head behind him. "I've got three boats blocking our dock, and I was supposed to get a delivery today."

Liam took a few steps forward and peered into the nearest boat. Crinkled beer cans and food wrappers dotted the floor.

"You didn't happen to see who left these boats, did you?" the foreman asked.

Liam shook his head. "They must've come in late last night. They were already here this morning."

"Typical," he sighed, lifting his phone to his ear. He held up a finger, a signal for Liam to wait. "Hey, Mackenzie?" He said into the phone, "We've got a problem."

He waved a goodbye and took off down the dock, his steps heavy and swift.

Liam stared at the boats. He had assumed they were allowed to be there. They looked like luxury boats, clearly good for partying.

It was funny to see the burly foreman calling Mackenzie for help. What was she supposed to do about it? Was she going to show up here?

Hopefully not. Liam would have to hide in shame. He'd hoped to never have to face her again after how he'd spoken to her at the tea shop in his grumpiest state.

He stood on the dock, filming the mess inside the boats, and within half an hour, the mysterious boaters had returned. They flip-flopped past Liam, laughing and yelling, ignoring him like a discarded beer can.

It would be easy to walk away. It wasn't his business. But then...he had some responsibility to this project, even if he didn't want to make a film about it.

*This is how it starts. This is how Russell manipulates you.*

He pushed the thought away and walked toward them. "Excuse me. Are these your boats?"

There were five men who, at first glance, appeared to be wearing a uniform—white, short-sleeved, collared shirts, differing only by slight variations in their colored stripes. Only one turned to look at him, quickly averting his gaze.

Two women walked past without a glance at him, their chins high, their eyes blocked with dark sunglasses.

Liam took a step closer. "Are you friends of Russell's?"

The other patrons loaded into the boats, but one man stayed on the dock. He turned and looked at Liam.

"Listen man, you need to relax. You being stressed out is stressing me out."

Liam looked over his shoulder. "I'm stressing you out?"

"Yeah, you. Just *relax*, man."

"I'm quite all right, thanks," he said. "But you need to move your boats."

He scoffed and hopped onto the nearest boat. "Okay, bud. Go back to England, have some beans and toast for me, yeah?"

One of the other men laughed.

Liam sighed. They were even dumber than they looked. He stood, debating what to do, when the buzz of a seaplane floated in.

He looked up. It was Joey, coming in for a landing. The plane made a splash, gliding on the water. Liam squinted. Mackenzie's face was in the passenger window, her glare visible even from afar.

*Oh, dear.* As much as he wanted to hide, he needed to see what happened next. He picked up his camera and focused on the plane.

# Six

S he wasn't a violent person, but if these dock-blockers were more friends Russell had forgotten to tell her about, Mackenzie was going to fly to Belgium and beat him over the head with a planner.

"I didn't think Bailey Jo would really show up," was Russell's first excuse. "And Liam – that one's on me. I thought he was coming *next* month, but this is better. He might shoot a documentary about Lottie, and hey! Maybe you guys can be friends."

Mackenzie had no need for friends. She needed to quell the deep, uneasy nausea that started as soon as she got out of bed. She needed to find a solution for the bags under her eyes, one that was more realistic than getting better quality sleep or drinking less coffee.

She needed Russell to finish shooting his stupid vampire romance movie so he could come back and deal with his own mess, so she could get back to her real life and work a stable job with sane people.

The only benefit of this whole fiasco was her mom getting to go to Europe. It was her first time overseas and apparently she was having the time of her life.

The rest of it was a major inconvenience.

Joey touched down on the water and turned to her. "I don't think I can get close to the dock. Maybe you can—"

"Pull up next to their boat. I'll jump on."

He laughed. "Good one."

"I'm serious. Can you do it?"

He raised his eyebrows. "I think I can do a float-by, but I don't want you to injure yourself."

"The only person I'm going to injure is *them.*"

The plane slowed, nearing the largest of the boats. Mackenzie popped her door open and perched, muscles tense.

"Ready, set..."

She jumped, flying through the air headfirst, landing on the deck on her forearms and with a grunt.

The pain was nothing compared to the feeling of flying she had for that one magnificent moment.

Mackenzie stood, dusting her elbows off.

"What was that?" A guy rushed toward her, pink sunglasses on his face and a neon green drink in his hand.

She cocked her head to the side. "Hi there. I'm Mackenzie."

"No shoes on the deck, *Mackenzie,*" he said, mouth hanging open. "Seriously."

"Well, you're *seriously* blocking my dock, so...that's on you."

A second guy appeared, flanked by two women. They could've been twins with their matching white swimsuits, their dark hair shining halfway down their backs.

The new guy lurched forward. "You can't just get onto our boat! You're harassing us."

Mackenzie took a step away from his hot, rancid breath. His eyes were red and he swayed as he stood. "I'm not harassing you. I'm telling you to move these boats. We've got supplies coming in today and the dock can't be obstructed."

One of the women snickered. "Get off our boat or we'll call the police."

*Resorting to threats!* So, not friends of Russell's, then.

Mackenzie reminded herself to take a deep breath and looked at the woman. Her long, purple fingernails were wrapped around her cellphone, the camera pointing directly at Mackenzie.

The last time she'd been filmed by someone like this was when she'd worked at Target in high school and someone tried to return a visibly stained pirate costume on November first.

"Please call the police," Mackenzie said, smiling. "Your boats will be impounded and auctioned off and I'll have peace again."

The first guy scoffed. "Are you threatening me? Do you know how much money I make in a day? It's more than you'll make in your lifetime."

"And you're so incredibly charming, too." She took a steady breath. "You've got fifteen minutes to move before I call Chief Hank myself and tell him to bring the tow boat."

Was there a tow boat? Mackenzie had made it up, but it got them to be quiet for the first time since she'd jumped on the boat.

Maybe the silence meant the little hamsters in their heads were running in their wheels. If there even were any hamsters.

It was best to leave with the last word. She would call Chief Hank anyway. He had real authority.

She took a step forward. Neither of the guys budged, so she shimmied between their shoulders. She was stepping off the boat and onto the dock when a sharp, cold chill ran down her back.

Mackenzie spun around. One of the women stood with an empty cup in her hand and a smirk on her face. "Oops!"

"Dude, not on the seats! Get a towel!" the red-eyed guy yelled. "Now!"

The sticky-sweet drink dripped down her back. Mackenzie straightened her posture.

"Fourteen minutes," Mackenzie said before turning back to the dock.

Liam towered above her on the dock, his hand outstretched. "Are you all right?"

She hoisted herself up and dusted off her hands. "I'm fine, thanks."

She walked down the dock. Liam followed.

"They were quite rude to you."

She sighed and pulled out her phone. "They were."

Thanks to Granny, she had Chief Hank's private number. She rang and he answered. "It's Hank."

"Hi Chief, it's Mackenzie. I'm on Stuart and some bros blocked our dock. I thought they might be friends of Russell's, but they're not friendly at all."

He laughed. "Do you need me to send the sheriff boat up to scare them off?"

"Maybe." She paused. An engine revved. "They might be leaving."

"Let me know if they don't."

"I will. Thanks."

She hung up and crossed her arms over her chest.

Liam squinted over the water. "Looks like you scared them well enough."

"All in a day's work." She turned and looked at him. "You look surprised."

"Well," he said slowly, "I just watched you jump from a moving plane onto a hostile boat."

"Oh." She paused. She shouldn't say it. She shouldn't antagonize.

But she was on a roll.

"Just the average day in the life of a nepotism hire," Mackenzie said airily.

He sucked in a breath, his eyes fixed forward. "You heard that, then?"

She turned away, walking off the dock and onto land. A flash of cold washed over her body – maybe the adrenaline leaving. Or maybe the ice cube that had gotten down her shirt.

She wiggled until it broke free. "I did."

He rushed after her. "I was clearly in the wrong and taking out frustrations that had nothing to do with you."

"Mhm." She stopped walking, but he didn't.

Liam nearly toppled her over. "Sorry."

"It's fine."

"No, I am truly sorry. We got off on the wrong foot, and it was my fault. Actually, maybe a bit of Russell's fault, but mostly mine—"

A laugh escaped her and she looked down at her feet. Amazing she hadn't lost a sandal on that dive.

He continued. "There was no excuse for it."

The first boat pulled out of the dock, the second close behind.

"Don't worry about it," she said.

She'd just wanted to get her jab in. She didn't want to solicit an apology from him. He must think she cared. How embarrassing for them both.

"I hope we can still be friends, if only because I'm terrified of your Rambo-level skills in dealing with boorish men."

"As you should be." She smiled. "Have a nice day, Liam."

She left him standing on the dock. It was time to find the foreman and give him the good news.

# Seven

The sea pen supplies arrived without further incident. Liam captured the scene from the hillside, painting the large ship just as it was – gray and industrial – though in his mind's eye, he envisioned the shore as it looked a hundred years ago, with a wooden ship's blinding white sails approaching, the trees and birds and seals unchanged.

His daydreams stopped when he noticed Mackenzie walking down the dock. He dropped his paintbrush and ran.

"Mackenzie!" he called out, breathless by the time he reached her.

She turned. "Hi, Liam. Everything okay?"

"I wanted to let you know I'll keep an eye out for the boaters. I'm here painting every day, and I can keep them from blocking the dock again."

She nodded. "Thanks. I appreciate it."

"Should I contact you? If I see them."

Her eyes scanned the water. "Sure. Call the tea shop. They'll get the message to me."

Before he could ask what he should do when the shop was closed, she walked off.

He winced. Frostiness noted. It wasn't undeserved. Liam was disappointed in himself for losing his patience the day they'd met. The grind of travel had gotten to him – plus his fear that Russell had scammed him into coming all the way out here.

He had truly been his worst self, and now he had to find a way to undo it.

For the next few days, he watched the water constantly. If any boats full of indignant partiers showed up, he'd be the first to report it. If he was extremely lucky, he might get to see Mackenzie jump from a plane again.

Unfortunately, he wasn't lucky. The boaters didn't return, and the little cove brimmed with peace and nature. The unrest stayed in his chest, saved especially for the quiet nights in his room.

He was used to living in remote places. Liam bounced between remote parks and artist colonies, though he'd had enough of sharing a bathroom with a dozen other people.

The quiet places were better for thinking. He could read books, catch up on podcasts, or watch movies. It was best to avoid scrolling the internet – it was a path to madness and depression – but he sometimes couldn't resist it.

Late one night, while mulling over his surly debut in Russell's circle, he stumbled onto a slew of videos from the San Juan Islands.

Most of them were from tourists – their favorite spots and hikes. Whale watching tours. One woman who'd posted a two-hour vlog of herself chasing after Bailey Jo Collins, whom she insisted she'd seen in Friday Harbor.

The shakiness of the camera on that one gave him motion sickness, but he found her to be so hilarious, he had to watch.

After he finished that one, a video popped up from Stuart Island: **Crazy woman forced her way onto our boat!**

His stomach sunk. Liam clicked the link and a box popped up, telling him he had to download the ChatterSnap app to watch it.

*Ugh.* A lot of the people at his last artist colony used the app to promote their work. Liam refused to. The apps were bad for him. He couldn't look away. He'd sit around all day, clicking, pictures and videos scrolling past his dull eyes as the life drained out of him. He wouldn't get any work done if he downloaded it.

But the video was linked in an article by the San Juan News, and if this was what he thought it was...

He downloaded the app, tapping play as soon as it finished.

"The *craziest* thing just happened to us on Stuart Island," a woman said, her voice slow and tinged with the vocal fry of a Valley Girl.

He recognized her immediately, though seeing her close up was jarring. Her lips were swollen and unnaturally smooth, her skin shiny like plastic.

"So my boyfriend, who is the CEO of ZenithGenius, just bought this beautiful property on Stuart Island. You can check my profile to see pictures from the parties we've been having— it is *amazing* here."

How old was this woman? Maturity-wise, she seemed like a teenager, but it was hard to tell. She could be anywhere from nineteen to forty-nine.

"We thought the people on the island were like, super friendly, but obviously not, because then we met *this* woman." A freeze-frame of Mackenzie popped up next to her head. She pointed a long fake nail at Mackenzie's face. "She literally jumped onto our yacht *like a crazy person*, screamed at us, threw a drink all over me and the Italian leather loungers, and then told us that we weren't welcome here! I found out she's working for Russell Westwood, which is just crazy. I'm sure his PR team won't be happy about her *literally* assaulting us."

Liam scoffed. No one was buying this, were they? He scrolled through the comments.

**Looks like someone's about to get fired!**

**That is crazy. I'm so glad you're okay!**

**Can't pay attention to the haters <3 <3 LOVE YOU!!!**

Liam tossed his phone aside. How were people so gullible? Were they willing to accept this woman's version of events just because she was the one telling the story? Hadn't they ever heard of an unreliable narrator...or read a book?

Even the local news featured the video with a silly headline, "Watch your boats this summer!"

Absurd. A waste of words.

He stood, grabbing his laptop, and took a seat at the desk in the corner of the room. He plugged in his video camera and uploaded everything he'd recorded in the last month.

Then, scrolling through, he found the footage from that day. It began with a shot of the plane floating in. It rumbled along, slow and steady, when suddenly a blurry mass flew from the plane and slammed into the boat's deck.

He smiled. He remembered her moving more gracefully. Maybe it was best to leave that part out.

Liam kept watching. The video showed Mackenzie speaking respectfully. The boorish drunks, even worse on film, bellowing at her, laughing. The thrown drink. Mackenzie standing tall.

He smiled. Time to fight fire with fire and, perhaps, find a way to make up for his rudeness earlier.

Liam tapped away on his computer, making an account on the sworn-off ChatterSnap app.

When forced to add a profile picture of himself, he added the painting of the plump seal, then quickly uploaded the video of Mackenzie's confrontation before copying the link to the snarky woman's original video.

"It doesn't seem that's quite how it went down..." he wrote, hitting **REPLY**.

Then he waited, his heart pounding in his ears.

Five minutes. Ten minutes. He kept hitting refresh, expecting someone to comment, or the woman to pop in to argue with him, but nothing happened.

After an hour of no response, he shut his laptop and picked up his paperback copy of *1984*. He made it two chapters before his eyelids grew heavy, and he set the book down and shut out the light.

When he woke the next day, the first thing he did was check the app. His comment had been deleted, which he'd expected, but the rest of the comments on the original video harassing Mackenzie were flooding in too quickly to be nixed.

**Hm are you sure she threw that drink?**

**Liar liar, pants on fire!**

There were dozens of links to his video. He clicked over to his profile – thirty thousand views! And he'd somehow collected a few thousand followers, some of them leaving comments on his painting.

**I am not being hyperbolic when I say I would die for that fat seal.**

**Where can I get a print?**

He rushed to respond – *the San Juan Island Farmer's market* – then sat back, biting a nail.

He could see why people spent so much time on these apps. Each comment popped a bubble of dopamine in his brain, inviting him to stay there, hunched over, scrolling for the rest of the day.

But the sun was coming up and Liam was too old to develop an addiction to his phone. He refused to do it.

He found a way to set a timer on the app – no more than twenty minutes a day. He posted two more of his paintings with the caption, *Catch me and my work at the San Juan Island farmer's market next week!*

Then he turned his whole phone off.

He stood and managed to get himself to the hilltop just as the sun peeked out.

# Eight

What did it matter if some strangers on the internet thought she was unstable?

Mackenzie didn't care. She couldn't care less, in fact! She was in her soldier era. She was a fighter. Shakespeare knew what she was about.

So what if people on ChatterSnap thought she was overly aggressive? So what if someone she'd never met said she had a big forehead indicative of a low IQ?

She knew it wasn't true. She had to stop reading the comments. It would blow over in no time and, besides, she didn't have a big forehead. It was perfectly average. She'd tried bangs and they weren't for her. She wasn't going back.

The tea shop was empty today. Totally dead. No one had come looking for her. That was a good thing, really. They were afraid to confront her, because they knew they were lying.

Mackenzie sat, staring at her laptop screen, wondering what shame looked like for someone like the boaters.

"Should I take your phone away?" Eliza asked.

Mackenzie shut her eyes. She didn't realize she had it in her hand. "Maybe."

"It's not healthy to keep looking at that stuff."

"I said maybe!" Mackenzie barked, gripping the phone tightly.

Without thinking, she clicked on the ChatterSnap app. It opened to the video, and she quickly closed it. She didn't want to read any more comments today.

"I wonder if Steve will see it," Mackenzie said.

"Your ex-boyfriend will definitely not see it. You're only a local sensation," Eliza said with a smile.

Mackenzie groaned. She didn't want to be any sort of sensation. "I know it's dumb, but I just don't want *him* to see it."

"Because you're embarrassed?"

"I'm not embarrassed," Mackenzie said. "But he'll think he's doing better than me and I can't have that."

"He thinks he's better than everyone," Eliza said.

"Yeah, well. He's not winning the breakup. I am." She took her phone and slapped it into Eliza's hand.

"Winning the breakup?" Eliza laughed. "That's not a healthy way to deal with any of this."

"I will deal with this however I want, thank you." She squared herself in front of the screen. She had to do the budget for the month and make sure they were on track. That was something to focus on. Not stalking the profile of the person who had called her a "Kraken Karen of the Salish Sea."

"Could dealing with it include apple cobbler with ice cream?" Eliza asked. "I'm about to pull the cobbler out of the oven."

Mackenzie shut her laptop. "Yes, I think that's a good way to deal."

Eliza laughed. "Great."

Mackenzie would get through this. Russell was to blame, really. She'd give him a call soon.

# Nine

That afternoon, Liam finished painting and spotted Joey unloading some passengers at the dock.

"What's the best way to get to San Juan Island?" he asked.

"I'll give you a ride. That's what I'm here for." Joey handed him a headset. "Missing civilization?"

"Something like that," Liam said. "I need to make amends with Eliza and Mackenzie after being rude last week."

Joey flipped a switch and the engine kicked on, propeller spinning in front of them. "I didn't hear about you being rude, but Eliza was afraid she might've offended you with their version of an English tearoom."

"Offended me?" He laughed. "Why?"

Joey shrugged. "She's never been to the UK, so she thinks they've got it all wrong."

"Reminds me a bit of my gran's house, actually," Liam said. "In a good way."

Joey winced. "Maybe keep that to yourself."

They took off and, within minutes, Liam found himself back on San Juan Island, staring up at the little tea shop under the blazing sun. Sweat beaded his forehead. He wiped it away and kept walking.

The tea shop looked so different than it had in his memory, standing against a solid blue sky, the sun casting glimmers off the water. Orange and purple wildflowers dotted the grass, blowing in the wind.

Had this all been here before? In his mind's eye, the tea shop stood tall and dark, like some sort of gothic castle, lit only by lightning. How had he gotten it so wrong?

Shame smoldered in his stomach like a lump of coal. He trudged up the hill.

Liam got to the front door and pushed it open. A bell jingled, and both Eliza and Mackenzie stood behind the front counter.

"Hello," he said with a nod.

Eliza's face lit up with a smile. "Liam! It's nice to see you again. How are you doing over on Stuart Island?"

"Quite well, thank you." He shifted his weight. "I, uh, wanted to apologize for my less than gentlemanly behavior on the night of my arrival."

"What!" Eliza shook her head. "You were a perfect gentleman!"

Mackenzie stared at him, narrowing her eyes. "I mean, I wouldn't go that far."

"Stop," Eliza hissed. "It's part of his *culture* to apologize profusely."

A hearty laugh escaped him. "Yes, that's true." He cleared his throat. "I was hoping to have a moment of your time, Mackenzie. It's about the unruly boaters."

She sighed. "Oh, you heard? They're accusing me of attacking them."

"Yes, and it was – well, honestly, pretty outrageous."

"I don't care." She raised her chin high. "I know Russell won't put any stock into it and it doesn't matter."

"What about his PR team?" Liam said with a half-smile.

Mackenzie laughed. "There is no PR team. I'm the PR team."

"Oh."

Mackenzie tilted her head. "You seem disappointed."

"Not disappointed, no."

She went on. "It's not going to affect the project, and I'm sure it'll blow over. Next time I'll just sink their ships."

Eliza shot her a look. "Mackenzie. You can't sink people's ships."

"Yes I can."

"You don't know how," Eliza said.

Mackenzie narrowed her eyes. "Then I will learn."

"I think you should offer a public apology," Eliza said, nodding.

"Apologize for *what?*" Mackenzie shouted. "I didn't do anything wrong! They blocked a private dock, and the one woman threw her drink at me—"

"That's not what I heard," Eliza said, grinning.

Mackenzie stared at her, her mouth open. "If you—"

"I don't think you need to apologize," Liam said, cutting her off. He stepped forward. "I may have found a solution. I did something, and...well, I wanted to help."

Mackenzie raised an eyebrow. "Help who? Me?"

"Why don't you discuss it over some tea?" Eliza suggested, eyes bright. "The Yorkshire again?"

He nodded. He didn't have any decent tea on Stuart. "Thank you."

Eliza darted behind a door, and Mackenzie turned to him. Her eyes were steel. "Do you want to take a seat?"

"Sure."

She led him into a different room than he'd seen before, one with tatami floor mats, paper screens, and cherry blossoms painted on the walls.

"Is this the Japanese tearoom?" he asked as they sat on cushions on the floor.

"It is. Granny designed the whole place back in the day."

"It's very charming."

"Thanks. I'll tell her you said that." She flashed a quick smile. "So, what's this idea you had?"

If she were willing to talk to him about it, she must not be as unconcerned as she was trying to portray.

"First off, did Russell tell you anything about me creating a documentary about Lottie's return?"

She sighed. "No. Why would he?"

"It wasn't set in stone," he rushed to add. "It was an idea he'd had, and I wasn't sure I'd be able to make something, so I didn't commit to it." He leaned in. "After seeing what you did – jumping off that plane and all – I realized I might have judged the idea prematurely."

She snorted a laugh. "I'm glad I could get you to change your mind, I guess?"

The next part was more delicate. He cleared his throat. "I'm telling you this for two reasons. One, so you might agree to let me spend some time following you and your operations around here."

She frowned. "Okay..."

"And two, to explain why I have this." He pulled his phone out of his pocket, unlocked the screen, and slid it across the table.

Mackenzie picked it up, her eyebrows knitting together. "Is this a video? Of me?"

"Yes. It was for the documentary, but it ended up being quite handy for ending a debate on ChatterSnap."

A smile spread across her face. "That is quite handy." Her eyes stayed focused, watching the video.

When it was done, she handed his phone back. "I have to say it's a relief to see that. People were piling on so much about how crazy I was that I'd started to believe that maybe I *had* been too forceful."

"And that maybe you had thrown that drink?"

She laughed. "Yeah. Sort of. It's strange. I questioned myself." Mackenzie sat back, sitting up straight. "I should never question myself."

He smiled. "Anyway, I posted this video on the app. Everyone who sided against you...? Now they can see the truth."

She whipped her phone out of her pocket and tapped, tapped, tapped. A hand went to her mouth. "Whoa. That's awesome."

"What was it Churchill said? A lie can get halfway around the world before the truth can get its pants on?"

Mackenzie laughed, her shoulders rising and falling. "Am I the one caught with their pants down in this situation?"

"In a purely metaphorical sense, yes."

"Okay, Liam. I'll hand it to you. This was helpful. Thank you." She let out a breath. "It feels like a weight came off my shoulders."

"Wonderful. So you won't mind me tagging along and filming your business with the sea pen, then?"

Her gaze settled on him, her hard eyes searching, scanning.

Plates clanged, muffled by the walls. Liam held his breath. He didn't need to do the documentary, but he needed to see more of her in action.

"Fine," she said. "I'll allow it, but only to protect my good name."

Liam smiled and bowed his head. "Of course."

"Next week, I'm going down to the aquarium to check on Lottie. You can come if you want."

"That would be brilliant."

Eliza swooped in with a tray of tea. It smelled heavenly.

"This tea is fantastic, thank you," Liam said.

He lifted a cup of tea to his lips. Mackenzie wasn't the only one with a weight off their shoulders.

Liam wouldn't muck it up again.

# Ten

As weird as it was for Liam to have randomly recorded her, Mackenzie was grateful. After he released his counter-video, the woman who'd claimed she was "crazy" quickly deleted her version of events and went back to posting long videos of herself picking outfits for the day.

Had Russell really asked Liam to make a documentary about Lottie? Mackenzie had a vague memory of Russell talking about *wanting* to do a documentary, but he'd never put any plans into place.

Then again, planning wasn't Russell's forte.

Mackenzie wasn't going to concern herself with it. Whatever Liam decided to do was between him and Russell. He'd been helpful insofar as she could now move on from that debacle and focus on what she needed to do: keep the sea pen project afloat until Russell got back and hired someone else.

There were two main goals she had with a lot of little details underneath. First, she had to make sure construction stayed on schedule and the sea pen would be ready for Lottie when it was time to move her out to the island.

That was easy enough. It involved a lot of calls, nagging, and making sure everyone was aware of what needed to be done.

The harder goal was dealing with money. Why did it always come down to money? Why did it make the world go 'round, even for killer whales?

It took Mackenzie two weeks to sort through the mess of invoices the old assistant had left behind. She was relieved to find out there was enough money in the Lottie account to cover invoices, but there wasn't much left over.

That was the issue. They had large expenses coming up for the project and no real income for the project. It was all based on donations.

The Blackfish Ball would be more important than she'd realized. It would be their last chance to fundraise and make sure they had enough to get Lottie here in August.

Mackenzie would get it done. She had to. Once Lottie was here safely, Russell would return and find someone else to coordinate things. Her good deed would be done, and she could move on with her life.

Where she'd move on, she had no idea. When she wasn't working on things for the sea pen, she applied to jobs. So far, she'd sent out thirty-six applications. Not a single one had responded.

The only lead she had was with Cameron at Opuluxe Escapes. He'd followed up after their meeting with an email asking her to come to the office.

At first, she hadn't planned on answering, but after a fiery day arguing with the lumber supplier, she thought it might be wise to talk to the only company who might give her a new job after this one.

She wrote back. "I can stop by Monday."

He answered a minute later. "Wonderful. See you then."

• • •

The Opuluxe Escapes office was near Seattle. Joey had to take the plane in for maintenance in the city, and he graciously offered to give her a ride.

She caught a cab to Fremont. The building was tucked between a brewery and a glass high rise on the Lake Washington Ship Canal. Mackenzie checked in at the front desk and spent ten minutes gazing through the window at the ships floating by.

"It's my favorite saleswoman!"

Mackenzie jumped when she heard him. "Hey!"

Cameron walked toward her, dressed in a cobalt blue suit, white shirt, and skinny black tie.

He had the style of someone working with high-end clients. Mackenzie could dress well, too. That could be a fun change from her old frumpy office clothes.

He stuck out his hand, grinning. "I hope you weren't waiting too long."

She accepted his handshake. Maybe she should've dressed up more? She didn't want to look too eager. "Not at all. There's a great view."

"Thanks so much for coming out. I know you're busy, so I won't waste your time. I can give you the tour and we'll talk about sales as we go."

At least she'd worn comfortable heels. "Sounds good."

The elevator stood waiting, its golden doors shining Mackenzie's reflection back at her.

"We're probably not as big as your last company, but we have a decent sales force and all the support you could want. Our team handles all the bookings and vendors. They're available twenty-four hours a day to keep the clients happy – which means you don't have to be on call."

"That's efficient."

The elevator dinged with a light, metallic sound, and the doors opened. Cameron motioned for her to go first, and she walked into the wide space. The far wall was entirely made up of windows, boasting an even more impressive view of the canal, and desks stretched as far as she could see. People worked and chatted in bunches and pairs.

Cameron led the way. "That's our booking department," he said with a nod.

A woman smiled back. "Hey, Cam!"

He winked. "Sales staff are scattered all over the office. You'd have a desk, of course, but no one is going to keep tabs on you. If you need to meet with clients or want to work from home, you've got the freedom to do that."

"Oh, nice." Her old job had insisted they work in the office. It was impossible to get promoted without showing your face at least fifty hours a week.

If she worked here, she wouldn't have to leave the island. Not that she was sure she wanted to stay, but it was nice to have the option.

A woman with a headset waved at Cameron. He waved back.

"What did your top salesman make last year?" Mackenzie asked.

He stopped walking and leaned in close. "That's an excellent question. I shouldn't be telling you this, but our top salesman – not me, unfortunately – cleared half a million in commissions."

Her mouth popped open. "Half a million selling boat rides?"

"It's not just boat rides. Polar cruises are one kind of trip we curate. We also do safaris, archaeological digs, Australian outback tours. You name it, we make it happen. We're dream makers, Mackenzie, and I can tell you're one of us."

She smiled, casting her eyes to a boat passing in the canal. "I'm not sure I'm much of a dream maker."

"Fine, you don't have to be. You're a heck of a salesman, though, and you have something no one else here has."

She turned back to him, eyebrow raised. "What's that?"

"You have an *in* with Hollywood."

She scoffed, but before she could respond, he added, "I'm sure you would never capitalize on knowing Mr. Westwood, but the thing is—you wouldn't have to."

"I don't think I follow," Mackenzie said.

He nodded toward a door. "Let's talk in my office."

She walked in. Cameron took a seat behind a handsome reclaimed timber desk. Mackenzie sat in a plush leather armchair, her eyes scanning the black and white photographs framed on the walls. Some were of beautiful scenes. Others were of smiling faces.

Was he married? No obvious pictures of a wife. No ring on his finger.

"Bailey Jo is recommending you to all her friends. I had to send them to my other salesman, and a few insisted they *only* wanted to work with you."

"Uh huh." She crossed her arms over her chest. "I definitely believe you."

He put his hands up. "I'm serious. I'm not trying to schmooze you here. I'll even tell you the names when we get out of the building." He glanced at his watch.

Mackenzie leaned in. It was a Rolex. Maybe a Daytona? That was a classic, but pricey. Twenty thousand? Maybe thirty thousand?

"I've got a reservation at the best sushi restaurant in town," Cameron said. "Would you want to join me?"

She bit her lip. Joey might be done working on the plane. She didn't want to keep him waiting...

He spoke again. "You've got to let me make my pitch. I think you could take this company to the next level, and I can't just let you walk out of here without considering my offer."

She tried not to smile, but who was she to argue with that? "Sure. Why not."

"Excellent. We'll take the company car."

They waited in the lobby. Mackenzie texted Joey, and he assured her he was not in a hurry to get back to the islands.

After three minutes, a black Mercedes-Benz S-class pulled up to the building.

"After you," Cameron said. "By the way, when you work for us, you're free to use any car from our fleet when meeting clients or working with vendors."

It was getting harder to pretend she wasn't impressed. "That's good to know."

"I know you might think it's pretentious," he said, joining her in the backseat, "but when you're dealing with people who expect the best, you have to present the best. I drive a Toyota, but if I showed up to meet some of our clients in that, they'd laugh me out of the room. I had a guy tell me he would think I wasn't good at my job if I didn't show up in a luxury car."

Mackenzie tried not to let her face fall too much, but she didn't like dealing with snobs. "That's a whole different level than what I'm used to."

No one at her old job even saw her car. Most of her effort was put into demonstrations and convincing companies the software she was selling would revolutionize their work. This was far more showmanship.

"You'll get used to it. Believe me."

They were dropped off outside of a black brick building with a single red door. A man rushed out to greet them, a white and red hat upon his head.

"Mr. Walters," he said, holding the door open. "It's so good to see you."

"Thank you. It's good to see you, too."

He bowed slightly. "We have your table ready."

The man escorted them past tables filled with diners to a small bar with two seats directly in front of the sushi chef.

"I always recommend the tasting menu," Cameron said, pulling out her chair. "Is that okay with you?"

"Sure," Mackenzie said, taking a seat. She scanned the menu. No prices.

Cameron smiled. "This is all on me, of course."

"Oh, I—"

"Well, on Opuluxe," he laughed, holding up a metallic credit card.

"Company card?" she asked.

He shrugged. "You love to see it, don't you?"

She'd never gotten a company credit card. Truth be told, she *would* love to see it.

For the next hour, the conversation flowed.

"I stumbled into this," Mackenzie confessed. "I'm only covering until Russell gets back."

"You have a knack for it, though. I swear, I'm not blowing smoke here. You're talented."

She looked down at the slice of red fish sitting atop the perfect mound of rice on her plate. "Thank you."

"And, after you're done covering, you're ready for a new job, right?"

"Yes. I'll be on the market, so to speak." She laughed.

He glanced over at her. The smile disappeared from his face. His eyes were so intense she had to look away, butterflies taking off in her stomach.

"On the market..." he repeated, smiling to himself.

She took a sip of sake. "Right now, I'm just trying to keep the sea pen's construction on time and prepare for the fundraiser we have coming up."

His eyes brightened. "A fundraiser?"

"We're calling it The Blackfish Ball. It wasn't supposed to be a big thing, but the last assistant stole a bunch of money, so...you know how that goes."

"Ah, that's unfortunate." He grimaced, setting his chopsticks down. "What does a guy need to do to secure an invitation to this ball?"

She tried to stop the smile spreading across her face, but it was pointless. "I suppose a donation would help."

"I suppose it would." He cleared his throat. "Anyway, I hope you enjoyed talking today as much as I did."

Mackenzie smiled. "It was certainly interesting."

"I don't blame you for playing hard to get." He looked away, grinning. "Promise me you'll at least think about it?"

He was exactly the sort of salesman she could never be. Mackenzie was too intense for it – the charm, the wit, the carefree conversation. It made any sale feel low stakes, even if it wasn't. The perfect way to avoid stressing a valuable client.

She had her own tricks, but she had to admit. He was effective.

Mackenzie smiled at him. "I promise."

# Eleven

The next time Liam saw Mackenzie, she was halfway sticking out of the seaplane window, waving her arms.

"Yoohoo!" she yelled. "Lottie Airlines welcomes you aboard flight zero zero one, service to Marine Magic Funland!"

Liam grinned from behind the camera. He'd been filming all morning, trying to capture the chirping birds and bumbling boats along the green backdrop of the island.

That peace was broken now – and, somehow, only improved.

"It's quite nice having a private plane to take you everywhere, isn't it?" Liam said as he got in the back.

"Not with this pilot," Mackenzie jerked her head to the side. "He's been mouthing off all morning. I'm going to have to fire him and get someone else."

"Ha!" Joey turned the engine on. "I'd like to see you try!"

Liam shook his head and buckled in.

It was a clear day. He sat back, catching incredible shots from the sky: the deep blue water speckled with lush green islands large and small; cliffs and bluffs and sandy shores; a huddle of seals on a rocky outcrop.

When they flew near Marine Magic Funland, he got a different sort of shot. Rows and rows of cars reflecting the sun in the blacktop lot. Looping, curling tracks of roller coasters. A round pool of bright blue water, a black whale stretched half-way across the surface.

They landed on a small airstrip near the park.

"I'm going to hang back," Joey said, shutting off the plane. "I don't need these people hitting me with a restraining order too."

Liam turned to Mackenzie. "Should I expect a restraining order?"

"No." Mackenzie paused. "Probably not. Are you worried about it?"

He smiled. "Not at all. I'm fairly certain your country's laws don't pertain to me. I only answer to King Charles."

Mackenzie stared at him for a beat. "Right."

"I'm kidding, of course. I don't even like Charles."

"Does anyone?" She cracked a smile. "The Marine Magic Funland people only went after my mom because she wrote the letter that set this whole thing off."

"I don't think Russell told me about any of it."

She sighed. "My mom's dad – my grandpa – was the one who accidentally caught Lottie in a fishing net and sold her off. My mom was just a kid when it happened, but it tormented her for years. Then, one day, she came to this park for work and walked right into her old friend."

"Wow. Do you think she'd be willing to sit for an interview?"

"Probably. She'll do anything for Lottie." She waved good-bye to Joey and started walking. "Russell was part owner of this park. There are three others – a guy and a couple. The guy came around to the idea of retiring Lottie to a sea pen. The other owners are still salty about the whole thing."

Liam nodded. "I see. And your mum – was she dating Russell at the time? When she found Lottie?"

"No. That's a whole thing. I don't think you have time for it in your documentary."

"So you're saying," Liam said, keeping a straight face, "it's a love story?"

"Yeah, sure." She rolled her eyes. "Anyway, you should be safe, but if you notice anyone coming at you with an open can of paint?" She made a face. "Duck."

"Will do," he said.

They got a ride to the park's front gate.

"We have to buy tickets to get in," Mackenzie explained as they approached a window.

"Are you serious?" Liam said. "I thought Russell was an owner."

"He is, but it's become hostile with those other two." She laughed and handed her credit card to the ticket agent. "Look," she waved him closer. "They've got my mugshot hanging in there."

Liam leaned in. She smelled of citrus and floral, clean and sharp. Her hair was tucked behind her ear, and she had such a delicate curve to her neck...

"See?" she said, pointing. "It must've happened after the last time I visited. Ha!"

He snapped his attention to the poster with her black and white photograph and the words **REPORT IMMEDIATELY TO MRS. SMITT.**

The checkout girl looked over her shoulder, then back at Mackenzie. "Oh! That *is* you."

"Guilty. I'm Mackenzie Dennet. Nice to meet you."

The girl's hand hung in the air, her eyes wide. "Do you get to work with Russell Westwood?"

"I do."

A smile spread across her face. "What's he like? Do you have any funny stories?"

Mackenzie reached to take her credit card back. "He's pretty funny, but he's also a lot nicer than you'd expect. Like, overly nice."

She grinned. "That's so cool."

"Have a great day!" Mackenzie said, stepping through the front gates. "And," she said in a low voice, "he's an annoying boss and a terrible planner, but we can't let the enemy know that."

Liam followed her and a man with a large camera approached them. "Would you like your picture taken?"

Mackenzie said, "No, thank you," just as Liam said, "Absolutely."

The flash popped, blinding them both. "You're number 187. You can purchase a copy at the stand over there."

Liam blinked, trying to find a corner of his vision that still worked. He could make out Mackenzie glaring at him.

"What do you think you're doing?" she asked.

"I wanted a picture for my mugshot. You don't get to hog all the glory for yourself."

She laughed. "Come on."

They wove through the park, gravel crunching underfoot as they passed walls of pink cotton candy and overstuffed whales hanging from stands. The sun felt more intense here— maybe from the lack of trees—and the screams of riders and the smell of frying oil hung heavy around them.

The whale stadium was tucked in the back of the park. Stairs led to the doors and paint was peeling from the handrails and walls. A pulldown metal gate blocked the entrance to the stadium, with a sign that read **NO PERFORMANCES SCHEDULED.**

"We can go around the side here. They're expecting us." Mackenzie walked to a door marked **DO NOT ENTER** and knocked.

It popped open and a woman peered out. "Mackenzie! It's so good to see you. Come on in."

"Hey, Inge. This is Liam."

He waved a hello and caught one last shot of the entrance over his shoulder before the door shut.

He followed them inside. The stadium was lined with empty benches, wrapped around the tank, stacked to the sky.

Front and center in the water was Lottie, her black skin glistening in the sunlight, her mouth open and water lapping over a row of pointed white teeth. She raised her head out of the water, rolling her tongue and making clicking sounds.

"Whoa," Liam whispered. He'd never seen an orca before, and certainly not this close.

Mackenzie and Inge chatted, but he couldn't hear anything they were saying. He floated toward the tank, his camera dropping to his side.

"Hello," he said softly when he reached the glass.

The waterline was at his eye level, and when he put his hand up, Lottie blew a misted breath in the air before ducking beneath the surface.

He leaned closer and Lottie turned on her side, looking at him for a moment. He smiled and a bubble blasted out of her mouth.

He jumped back, stumbling, before bursting into a laugh.

"Lottie likes to joke around," Inge said with a grin.

"She's unbelievable." He walked back to the glass and put his hand near her nose.

She blew another bubble, then opened her mouth wide.

"It looks like she's laughing at me," he said, laughing himself.

"She is," Mackenzie said. "She's like, 'I got you so good!'"

His entire torso could fit into her mouth. Her tail was two car lengths away.

"She's beautiful," he said softly.

"She is," Mackenzie took a deep breath. "Inge, Liam is working with Russell to make a documentary about Lottie's rehabilitation and release."

"It's nice to meet you!" Inge said. "Thank you for doing this."

"The pleasure is all mine," he said, tearing his eyes away from Lottie for the briefest of moments. "I'd love to talk to you about this process, maybe get something on film?"

"I'd love to! Right now, I spend about half my time here and the rest in the San Juans. We've been training Lottie to hunt fish. Her progress is blowing us all away! She's been nabbing salmon in seconds, which is a huge improvement from before, when she kept playing with them."

A voice boomed over the loudspeaker. "Mackenzie Dennet. You are to leave the premises immediately."

Mackenzie rolled her eyes. "Here we go."

A metal door clanked open, and a woman dressed head to toe in a lavender pantsuit emerged from the top of the stadium. Her shoulders were slightly stooped and she walked holding the arm of the large man at her side. Her chin stayed high and her eyes pulled narrow.

Liam picked the camera up and framed her in the center. This was going to be good.

# Twelve

Her mom had warned her about this, but Mackenzie was still having a hard time keeping a straight face.

"Hello, Mrs. Smitt," she said. "Nice to see you again."

"You're not supposed to be here." Mrs. Smitt stopped a foot from her face, pointing a finger at her nose. "This time I've got backup."

Mackenzie glanced at the man standing next to Mrs. Smitt. His black T-shirt looked painted onto his skin, bunching up at the biceps and lifting over his rounded belly. His black cargo pants had more pockets than she could count, and his scowl was deep and theatrical.

It was hard to feel afraid of the man but, to his credit, he was a head taller than Mrs. Smitt, and at least two Mrs. Smitts wide.

"Why would you need backup? This isn't a battlefield," Mackenzie said. "Mrs. Smitt, when you and your husband sold your interest in Lottie to Russell, you forfeited the right to—"

"My husband was the one who wanted that deal, not me!" she snapped. "We were tricked. We sold her for next to nothing. How was I supposed to know Lottie was about to become the most popular whale in the world?"

Back to money. Of course.

Mackenzie took a breath, keeping her tone steady. "Lottie is only popular because of what Russell is doing. If you'd kept her performing as you were, she would've cost you millions in vet bills and tank repairs."

"Well, you're not allowed to be here!" She stomped her foot. "I mean it!"

"When I'm done checking in with the staff, I'll be on my way."

Her eyes scanned Liam, up and down. "Is this skinny little guy the best Russell could get for your protection?"

Liam didn't flinch, keeping the camera on her. Mackenzie could see a smile flicker on his face.

"I don't need protection, Mrs. Smitt," Mackenzie said calmly. "I'm here to work. Not to fight."

Inge handed her a pen and a clipboard stacked with papers and she flipped through them, marking as she went along.

"Well, *I'm* here to fight," Mrs. Smitt said.

This was the second time Liam had filmed Mackenzie, and the second time she was fighting with someone. The documentary would just be a montage of her fighting people.

Soldier era indeed.

Mackenzie bit her lip. "I'm not doing anything wrong. If your friend wants to pick me up and throw me out of the park, that's one thing. For now, I'm going to talk to Lottie's trainers and plan her transfer in a few weeks."

Mrs. Smitt said nothing, standing with fists clenched. For the next hour, she and her tight-shirted friend followed at a distance as Mackenzie went through plans with the veterinarians and the transport teams.

It had been Russell's idea for her to do an in-person check-in. Mackenzie had resisted at first, but now she could admit he had been right. They were able to catch two potential issues just talking through plans, and everyone had a chance to bring up concerns in person.

Getting to see Lottie was another plus. It was easy to lose sight of their goal when people were trying to fight her every other day, but being able to look Lottie in her beautiful, soulful eyes set Mackenzie's mind straight.

When they were done, Mrs. Smitt followed them as they walked out of the park.

"It must make her feel triumphant," Liam noted, standing on the other side of the gates, still recording.

Mackenzie could only roll her eyes. "Whatever makes her feel better."

He turned, narrowing his eyes. "Look. She's still glaring at you."

Mackenzie snorted a laugh. "Liam! Don't instigate her."

"Come on, this is great. 'Angry woman in front of dilapidated roller coaster shakes fist.' Could be our opening shot. Who knows?"

She shook her head and pulled out her phone. There was a text from Joey.

**Needed to make a quick side trip to pick up another passenger – hope you don't mind. Maybe grab some lunch?**

Worked for her. She wrote back. **We'll get you something**.

His reply came quickly. **YES!**

Presumably, Russell paid him a salary, but Mackenzie suspected he'd be happy trading his services for cakes and roasts.

She turned to Liam. He was still filming and had a grin plastered on his face. "Joey had to make a detour. Do you want to get lunch somewhere?"

"Sure." He turned, pointing the camera at her.

"One thing," she said, holding up a hand. "You have to put that away. I feel like there's a third person with us all the time."

"There sort of is, if you count Mrs. Smitt."

She pursed her lips. "Liam. I'm serious. It's like...I don't know. You're using the camera as protection. A barrier. Like there's a wall between you and the world. We can't have a conversation because the camera is always there."

Liam tutted, turning the camera on himself. "I've just been accused of being closed-off and unfeeling. Unbelievable."

Mackenzie laughed. "I didn't say anything about unfeeling. I'm sure your sensitive artist heart beats behind the lens."

Liam dropped the camera to his side. "That's quite enough, thank you. I don't need you breaking through my psyche."

He put the camera away and they walked through the parking lot, hot cars baking on the asphalt. Traffic blasted by on the street ahead of them, a slim sidewalk at the edge.

Mackenzie's stomach rumbled and sweat sprouted on her forehead. All this arguing was getting to her. She needed to replenish.

"I can see a little diner over there. Does that work for you?"

He nodded. "Sure."

They walked to a traffic light and hurried across four lanes to get to the little building. It was the size of a double-wide trailer, with windows along the side.

They walked in and cold air hit her like a wall. Whole pies stood in glass stands, casting rainbows in the sun. Sweat slid down Mackenzie's back as they sat at a booth with a red table-top. The only other patrons were two men seated on round yellow barstools.

"I hope you weren't expecting American fine dining," Mackenzie said as she ran a hand over the table. Her hand only stuck to one spot. Not bad.

She unfolded the menu and hid behind its massive pages.

"I'm not a snob, if that's what you're wondering," he said. "I spent a year living off MREs."

A picture of a salad stared back at her. A salad wasn't going to cut it. She flipped to the burgers. "Why would you do that?"

"I was working as a tour guide in South America. I led people on weeks-long backpacking trips."

Mackenzie blinked. It was too much to read. A burger would do.

"Really?" She set her menu down and looked at him. "*You* did that?"

He glanced up at her and smiled. "Is that a tone of disbelief?"

"I just assumed you went to Oxford or something and lived on a three-thousand-acre estate while waiting to inherit your title as duke."

He lifted an eyebrow. "I think you've watched too much TV."

"You might be right."

"I didn't go to Oxford. I grew up in Cambridge, but I didn't go to school there. It's quite prestigious, you know, and I'm not very smart. Or wealthy."

She laughed. "Could have fooled me."

His eyes darted above his menu. "I went to the University of Nottingham for film. You know how the river runs through the town in Cambridge?"

"Yes," she lied.

"My family owns a punting business there. That's what I grew up doing – giving tours on the river. After college, I spent time filmmaking, but that went south. I left in search of adventure."

"How did filmmaking go south?"

"Speaking literally, I ended up in South America and grew adept at bribing officials."

Her mouth popped open. "No way!"

"Yes." He set his menu down and folded his hands on the table. "I am not, in fact, part of the landed gentry, but I know how to keep a bunch of backpackers safe."

She kept a straight face. "That's disappointing."

"You're telling me."

"I was asking about the filmmaking, though. What went wrong?" She sat back and crossed her arms over her chest. "Or do you need to hide behind the camera to be able to talk about it?"

He grinned. "I'm not hiding."

"It seems like hiding."

The waitress stopped by and got their orders – a cheeseburger and fries for Mackenzie, and meatloaf with mashed potatoes and corn for Liam.

"Meatloaf?" Mackenzie mouthed as the waitress walked off.

"Sounds like a delicacy," he said. "I had to try it."

Mackenzie grimaced. "It's going to be an experience, I'm sure."

He took a sip of water, set the red plastic cup down, then looked her in the eyes. "I made a few small films when I was at school."

His gaze was so focused it made her heart rate quicken. "Anything I'd know?"

Liam smiled and shook his head. "No."

"Ah." Mackenzie looked down at her cup of water.

Maybe she shouldn't force people to talk about themselves if they didn't want to. It was too hard to tell if he was annoyed. He always had the same intense look on his face, like he was solving a math problem. He was probably seething under there.

"There's this idea for new filmmakers to not wait to make something. They call it a micro budget film. I made one using the entirety of my savings. We were going to shop it around the local film festivals, try to make a name for ourselves."

She looked up. "What happened?"

He pushed his cup to the side and leaned forward, his hands clasped in front of him. "It didn't work out."

"Forgot to pay the right bribes?"

He grimaced. "Completely. They sent me to Australia for my crimes."

Mackenzie laughed. "Okay, you got me on that one."

"Thank you. I try." He sat back with a smile on his face. "What was your story before becoming the muscle on this project?"

"The muscle." She scoffed. "I sort of am, aren't I?"

"Mrs. Smitt had no idea who she was dealing with."

She wanted to be more witty, but she was so hungry she was getting dizzy. "Clearly."

Their meals arrived. Mackenzie's looked like it had come out of a burger catalog – a perfectly fluffy bun, centered cheese, ripe red tomato slices.

Liam's was a plate of brown, swimming in gravy.

When the waitress walked away, he leaned in close and looked up at Mackenzie. "What have I done?"

She stifled a laugh. "I'm not really sure."

He shook his head and picked up a fork and knife.

Mackenzie covered her mouth, trying to contain a bite of burger as the suppressed laugh escaped her. "You might like it."

He cut a small piece and took a bite, chewing. "Hey. That's not half bad. It may *look* like cat food, but in actuality, it's…"

"Dog food?"

He smiled. "Yes. An unidentified brown meat that came out of a tin with a dog on the label." He popped his fork into the mashed potatoes. "These are quite nice."

She set her burger down. "That's good."

"It seems like you're avoiding my question," he said, waving a meatloaf-laden fork at her. "Do you have something to hide, Mackenzie?"

A chill ran down her back. The heat was finally dissipating. "I'm not avoiding it. I was just really hungry."

He stared at her, then snapped his eyes back to his plate. "I've lost my appetite."

Mackenzie smiled and took a sip of water. "Before I got tricked into being Russell's temporary assistant, I worked in sales. Software."

"Ah. Very respectable, but doesn't explain your skills in jumping from moving planes."

She rolled her eyes. "That's just a lot of gymnastics growing up. And Pilates now."

"Hm."

"I had to leave my last job because my boyfriend worked there too and...things fell apart between us."

That was the smoothest she'd been able to tell someone about her horribly nasty breakup. Maybe she was healing.

"I'm sorry. That's a terrible way to go."

"Don't pity me." She picked up a fry and chomped on it. "How awful is it that I'm realizing I never even liked that job?"

He shrugged. "Doesn't seem uncommon."

"But I *thought* I did. It's because I'm competitive. They knew how to wind me up." She had another bite of burger. It was the best burger she'd ever had, she was sure of it.

Her blood sugar had to be soaring with glee, because she couldn't stop talking, even with her mouth full. "The only time I was ever happy, I think, was when we all went to a conference in Hawaii."

"Sounds like a place to fall in love."

Mackenzie puffed out her cheeks. "It was. That was where we started dating, in Kauai. It was heaven on earth."

"I've never been," he said.

"You should go. Anyway," she waved a hand, "I am definitely winning the breakup."

He laughed. "Is that what you're supposed to do after a breakup?"

"Yeah, Liam, keep up! I left that job and went *directly* to saving a whale. You can't dream up that sort of career advancement."

"Are you saving her, or is she saving you?" He stuck out his lower lip in a pout.

"Oh, shut up!" She threw a fry at him. "I'm just trying to do the right thing."

He took the fry and ate it. "No one does the right thing."

"I'm saving *her*, thank you. Then I'm going to land a way better job and show him he made a huge mistake."

"Sounds like a plan." He paused. "Just don't fall in love with your coworker again."

She rolled her eyes. "Who said I was in love? This is about winning, Liam. Focus."

"I am focused! Winning. Got it." He took another bite of meatloaf, then set his fork down. "Okay, I can't take any more of that. It's like eating a sponge."

She laughed. Maybe Liam could make some connections at the Blackfish Ball and restart his film career. Normally, she didn't like people schmoozing on Russell's Hollywood connections, but with Liam, she didn't think she'd mind.

Maybe Cameron would come to the ball, too. Had he been serious about attending?

If she decided to work at Opuluxe Escapes, he wouldn't *technically* be her boss. They'd be coworkers. That was different than her last job, right?

No. She wasn't falling into that mess again, and even daydreaming that it was a possibility was a pointless vanity. She had to get that under control.

She pushed her plate toward him. "Have some fries. Joey won't like you getting sick on his plane."

"Thank you. Very kind."

She would stay focused, too. No more daydreaming about Cameron. There was a ball to plan.

# Thirteen

The quiet life was waiting for Liam when he got back to Stuart Island. He was happy to ease back into it, combing through footage and posting his paintings on the Chatter-Snap app.

If anonymous online avatars were to be believed, there were at least ten serious buyers planning to come to the farmers market the next week.

He had seven new paintings completed, but whenever he sat down to paint the eighth, every brushstroke went wrong, the colors refused to blend, and the canvases ended up in the garbage.

It felt like he couldn't see what was right in front of him. He dumped the latest attempt, then pulled out a new canvas just as Joey's plane pulled up to the dock.

Liam stood from his seat so quickly he knocked the easel to the ground.

"Morning, Joey!" he yelled as he approached the plane.

Joey was bent over, tying the plane to the dock. "Hey man!"

Liam peered through the windows of the plane. There didn't seem to be any passengers. "How are you?"

"Good! Did you see me trying to get to the dock? I kept getting pulled back out."

"Ah, I didn't. I've got my head in the clouds, I guess."

He waved a hand. "It was wild. The water looks calm, but there's a crazy current. Anyway. How are you doing? Did you get your restraining order yet?"

"Not yet." Liam held up his hand, fingers crossed. "Here's to hoping."

Joey laughed. "I'm surprised you walked in there voluntarily. Did you really record Mrs. Smitt yelling at Mackenzie?"

"Oh yeah. That was great stuff."

"I have to see it."

Liam nodded up the hill. "Have you got a minute? I'll show you. I haven't had a chance to review it yet."

"Yes!" Joey said, grinning.

They got to Liam's room and he loaded the video onto his laptop. He started playing as Mrs. Smitt walked down the stadium stairs. Joey hummed The Imperial March and Liam burst into laughter.

By the time Mrs. Smitt started yelling at Mackenzie, both of them were bent over, tears streaming down their faces.

"Okay, okay, stop," Joey said. "I can't take it. This is hilarious."

Liam paused it and let out a slow breath. "Whew. Sorry. I don't know why it's so funny."

"It's the rage on her face. She's so small, yet so angry."

Liam paused the frame on Mackenzie. "I really enjoy the bored expression on Mackenzie's face."

"The clipboard!" Joey said, pointing. "Where did she get that? Is it a prop?"

Liam felt himself starting to slip into laughter again. "No, someone gave it to her. She was checking things and ignoring the glare."

Joey stood, wiping tears from his eyes. He walked to the far side of the room where Liam had stacked paintings.

"This looks like a decent place to stay," Joey said. "Did you paint all of these?"

Liam shut the laptop. "Yeah."

Joey sifted through the canvases. "Whoa. Is this my plane?"

"Yeah. I paint whatever is around. You can have it, if you want."

Joey held it in his hands, his wide eyes scanning back and forth. "Really? It's awesome."

"It's yours."

"How much do I owe you?"

Liam shrugged. "How about a ride to the tea shop?"

Joey tucked the painting under his arm. "Deal. I'm supposed to fly one of the contractors back in like thirty minutes."

"Works for me," Liam said.

They walked back down to the plane and waited.

"Where are you staying?" Liam asked.

He winced. "Russell was going to rent a place for me, but he ended up letting me use one of the rooms in his house in the meantime. I've just never left."

Liam narrowed his eyes. "Are you kidding me right now? I'm staying in a studio in the middle of nowhere, and you're in a mansion?"

"I'm sure if you wanted to, you—"

A smile broke Liam's scowl. "I'm kidding. Totally kidding. I love it here."

Joey let out a breath. "You almost got me. You're good at not breaking character."

He wanted to find a segue into talking about Mackenzie, but it was too awkward. Instead, he said, "Thanks."

. . .

The flight was quick, and soon Liam stood in front of the place that clouded all his thoughts.

"Maybe I'll set up out here," he announced.

Joey had a hand on the front door of the tea shop. "At least come in and get something to eat."

Mackenzie's car wasn't in the parking lot. What was the point of going in? She might still be inside, though. Maybe her car stayed at her granny's place...

He followed Joey in. Eliza was at the register, and she broke into a grin when she saw Joey. "Hey there handsome."

"Why hello, little lady." He leaned an elbow on the counter. "What's cookin'?"

Liam stayed back by the door. "Hello."

"Oh, hey Liam!" Eliza leaned to look past Joey. "Interested in a lemon rhubarb scone?"

"Sounds delicious." He cleared his throat. "I was thinking of setting up outside to paint the tea shop, if that's all right?"

"Yes! Please do. Granny would love it. She's at the cottage right now, but maybe I could buy it from you for her?"

"If it's half decent, you can have it for free."

She waved a hand. "No, I will definitely pay for it. I can bring you some tea outside, too. Do you need a table or anything?"

"No, I've got everything I need, thanks. I'd love to try the raspberry tea."

"I'll bring out a pot!"

As he set up his easel, he positioned himself in front of the tea shop so he could capture the view of the sea behind it. The sky was a wall of solid blue today. It would be a good place to start.

He mixed in a touch of white and made the first dabs on the canvas. Liam stood back, staring. A touch more gray, maybe, to balance the hue.

That did the trick. Then he moved onto the tea shop. The old wooden boards were painted a beautiful seafoam color. He made sure to note the position of the sun and the shadows. It looked perfect in this light, like something out of a storybook.

The painting was turning out all right, but it was impossible to capture the magic of the place or the electric zing he felt every time he looked over his shoulder, sure Mackenzie was about to pull up.

He was painting the windows on the tea shop when he heard a "Hey!"

Liam jumped. How had she snuck up on him? "Mackenzie. Hi."

She gasped. "Liam! I didn't know you painted things too."

He took a step back. "Did you think I sat at the top of the hill just to spy on everyone?"

"I mean, I didn't know you were *good* at it." She smiled at him, squinting against the sun. "This is really nice."

"I'm glad you like it."

Maybe a cloud would do some good. The sun was beating onto him now, his heart beating too fast, his skin growing hot.

"It's a magnificent day, isn't it?" she said, tilting her head.

The intense sky lent blue to her normally gray eyes. She smiled up at him, grinning, really scrunching her nose when she said, "Magnificent."

"It is," he managed to say.

"I don't want to interrupt you. Enjoy the day!" She walked past him, pausing at the tea shop door for a moment and staring at the sea.

Her outline was dark against the water, and she stood with one hand on her hip and the other to tame her hair in the wind.

She turned around, still squinting. "The water's so calm today. I wish I could go out and enjoy it."

"Yeah," was all he managed to say.

He watched her as she slipped inside the tea shop, his stomach churning.

The water only looked calm at the surface, but of course, he wasn't going to correct her.

# Fourteen

It wasn't strictly necessary for Cameron to make the trip to Stuart Island, but the benefits outweighed the hassle. The scenery was great, and the researchers were thrilled to finalize plans for their luxury cruise with Bailey Jo.

Seeing Liam again was a curveball. The tea shop was one thing – that seemed like bad luck – but after spotting him painting away at the hill overlooking the docks, it seemed like Liam was following him.

But how? And to what purpose?

Thankfully, Cameron managed to avoid being spotted. He waited until Liam was out of sight to return to the seaplane.

"Until we meet again, nutcase," he muttered, slamming the door shut.

Opuluxe Escapes had been happy to charter a private flight for him. He was pulling in so many star clients that his boss said they were considering opening two new offices, including one in LA that he'd be in charge of.

Enough of the dreary clouds of the Pacific Northwest. It was time for his turn in the sun.

"Do you mind making a short detour?" he asked the pilot. "I need to make one last drop."

They flew into Friday Harbor and Cameron caught a ride to the tea shop with a friendly woman he'd met near the docks. The parking lot of the little shop was empty this time around, devoid of prying eyes.

He walked in and spotted Mackenzie sitting at a table with a laptop and stack of papers.

"It looks like I just walked into a command center," he said.

She spun around, her eyebrows bunched until her eyes settled on him.

Then, she smiled. "I'm a busy woman, Cameron."

He slid into the seat across from her. "I see that. Do you mind if I join you for a moment?"

She turned her eyes back to her screen. "If you're trying to pressure me, it's not going to work. I still have a few weeks left here and there's literally no one else to do the work."

"Yeah, you mentioned that. Is it the Blackfish Ball?"

"I've got it up to *here* with this ball," she said, chopping a hand to her forehead.

He snapped his fingers. "That reminds me." He put a hand into his suit pocket. "I've come with news."

"Something hand-delivered by Opuluxe Escapes, eh?" She took the check from his hand and slowly unfolded it, her eyes stopping at the number. "Well. That is very generous."

"Anything for the whales."

"I didn't know Opuluxe cared about whales."

He smiled. "Just this whale, to be honest."

Mackenzie tucked the check away and smiled at him. "Thank you. That's very kind."

An older woman in an apron walked to their table. "Who's your friend, Mackenzie?"

"Granny, this is Cameron from Opuluxe Escapes."

"Oh, that's right!" She shook her head. "Sorry, sonny, my eyesight's not what it used to be."

He stood and offered a handshake. "Lovely to meet you again! This tea shop is incredible. A real gem."

"It is, isn't it? What are you drinking?"

Cameron puffed out his cheeks. "I'm not a big tea drinker, to be honest."

"How about an iced tea?" Granny suggested. "I can get you some maple bacon cookies, too."

"I can't say no to that."

She smiled. "Right answer."

He cleared his throat and took his seat. "Your grandma is adorable."

Mackenzie peered over her screen. "Don't be lulled into a false sense of security. She's scrappy, and you can't turn your back on her."

A younger woman appeared at their table. "Mack! You didn't tell me you were having company today."

"I didn't know," she said.

"Hi, I'm Cameron."

"I remember. I'm Eliza, Mackenzie's sister."

He put a hand to his forehead. "Yes, of course. We met when that swarm of people came after Bailey Jo."

"That's right! How is she?"

"She's well. Planning a trip to see some icebergs."

Mackenzie cleared her throat. "Eliza, I think Granny needs some help."

Eliza frowned. "Granny's here?"

"Yeah, she's buzzing around, forcing iced tea on people."

Eliza winced. "Oh. I'll go check on her."

Cameron turned his attention back to Mackenzie. "What's the dress code for the ball? I would check my invitation, but I don't remember getting one."

A grin spread across her face. "I'm so sorry for the oversight. Our party planning committee is short staffed."

"No apology necessary."

"The ball is black tie."

"Not black tie *and* black and white?" he asked. "Seems like a missed opportunity for a black and white whale."

"You're free to wear whatever colors you like," she said.

"Ah, so I *am* invited! Funny how these things work." He smiled, standing from his seat. "Give your granny my apologies. I've got a plane waiting in the harbor."

"No problem." She nodded toward the door. "Actually, you can tell him to meet you here and use our dock."

"Thank you, that's helpful." He stood. "Remember to save a dance for me, will you?"

She sat back and stared at him, a smirk on her lips. "I'll see what I can do."

He winked and walked out, a grin on his face.

# Fifteen

The moment the tea shop door shut behind Cameron, Mackenzie braced herself. The bells on the door jingled their little song, and Eliza burst out of the kitchen.

"What did he say?" she asked.

"He left without his tea and cookies." Granny had followed, a plate in her hands. Her lips twisted into a scowl.

Mackenzie glanced down at the check. Her head was lighter than her body, floating up, up, up... "He brought a donation for the Blackfish Ball."

Eliza wiped her hands on her apron. "Aw, that's sweet!"

"Why would he agree to cookies and tea, then just leave?" Granny snatched the check off the table before Mackenzie could react. "Ten thousand dollars!"

Eliza gasped. "What!"

"It's not from him, it's from the company," Mackenzie said. She put her feet flat on the floor. "I guess he really wants me to work for them."

Granny raised an eyebrow. "Are you sure that's all he wants?"

Mackenzie shut her eyes. "Granny!"

"I'm just saying!" She set the plate of cookies on top of a stack of papers. "A good-looking young man doesn't get all dressed up and come to a tea shop if he isn't trying to woo a young lady. Especially if he doesn't have any tea."

Eliza laughed. "I think Granny might be on to something, Mack."

"Of course I'm on to something. Not that anyone is going to listen to me." Granny cackled a laugh.

"It's not about listening, Granny," Mackenzie said, clicking extra hard on her computer. "I'm not interested in a romantic relationship, especially one with a potential coworker."

"Then why are your cheeks all flushed?" Eliza asked.

"And why won't you look me in the eye?" Granny added.

Mackenzie turned, eyes bulged, and stared at her. "There. Are you happy?"

Eliza shot Granny a look and they both erupted into snorted laughter.

"It's okay to admit you like him," Eliza said. "He is your type."

Mackenzie sat back. "I have a type?"

"Well, you know. He's just…"

Mackenzie leaned in. "What?"

She sighed. "This isn't an indictment of you, Mackenzie, but you're not the most approachable woman. The guys you end up with tend to be the ones with, you know, confidence."

Granny nodded. "Good looks, too. Like I said. That was a nice suit, wasn't it? The boys don't dress like that anymore."

"He was here for work, Granny." Mackenzie shut her laptop. "Thank you both for this riveting conversation. I'm going to the bank to deposit this into Lottie's account."

"Oh! I'll drive," Granny said. "I'm headed into town."

Eliza turned to her. "What for? I can go."

Granny stared at them. "I didn't have time to update you two, but your Aunt Adelaide moved her visit up. I need to pick her up from the ferry."

Mackenzie sat up. "What, is Aunt Addy coming *today?*"

"Yes. Your mom talked to her a week ago, and she sounded so down about being alone for her birthday that we pulled some strings to move her flight up!"

"Aw, poor Aunt Addy," Eliza said.

"You'll need to make space for her at the ball," Granny said. "And don't you dare make her feel unwanted!"

Mackenzie put her hands up. "I would never make Aunt Addy feel unwanted!"

It was bad enough that her husband had announced he wanted a divorce out of nowhere last year. Then, last month, she was laid off from her job as a professor.

Mackenzie could relate, somewhat. Though she'd technically been fired.

"Good," Granny said. "I'm picking her up in an hour. I can take you to the bank."

It seemed Mackenzie's plan to get away from their prying eyes failed. She pulled out her phone and saw she had a message from Cameron. Her heart leapt.

**I just had an idea as I was leaving the island. How would you feel about me inviting Bailey Jo to the ball? I'm not sure if she'd want to come, but it might be good publicity.**

Mackenzie's jaw dropped. "Cameron just said he could invite Bailey Jo to the ball."

Eliza shrieked. "Are you serious? Tell him to do it!"

"There had still better be room for Adelaide!" Granny barked over her shoulder as she walked off to the kitchen.

"There will be!" Mackenzie yelled back.

"Answer him!" Eliza said, nudging her. "I can redeem myself after acting like such an idiot in front of her last time."

"You weren't an idiot," Mackenzie said. She took a deep breath and wrote back.

**That would be incredible! Thanks, Cameron.**

She put her phone away, her heart still fluttering against her ribcage like a little hummingbird.

Maybe the job at Opuluxe wasn't what she wanted. Granny might be right. She often was.

Maybe Cameron was the prize? What better way to win the breakup than to level up? *Way* up?

"I was already so excited for this ball," Eliza said. "Now I'm not going to sleep at all."

Mackenzie bit her lip. "Me too."

# Sixteen

S even years without seeing the ocean. Adelaide stood on the deck of the ferry, her hands aching from clutching the railing so tightly.

The sun was strong today, but the wind was stronger. Her ponytail whipped in the gusts. Other passengers came out to take pictures before quickly retreating into the warm safety of the cabin.

She could follow them and get a soda. Her throat was still raw from the cold she'd caught a week prior. Maybe the caffeine would help, too. Not that she felt tired. This was the most excited she'd felt in months.

Her ex-husband Shane always had a hard time making this trip. He'd complained it was too long – an eight-hour flight from Ottawa, including the layover. On top of that was customs, and packing, and the stress of getting to the airport, and the cramped accommodations at her dad's house.

Shane was never a great traveler. He liked life the way he liked it. Smooth. Undisturbed.

Until, of course, he didn't.

Adelaide knew she had to take responsibility for her life. She could have come to visit if she really wanted to. In truth, she didn't even resent Shane in the moment. Right now, she missed having someone to share the mundane moments of her life with. No one else cared how long her cough had lasted and how many boxes of tissues she'd gone through. There was no one else who would make her tea with honey.

No one to tell how mist sprung to her eyes when she caught sight of Friday Harbor in the distance.

The pictures Sheila had sent were beautiful, but this? The shops on the hillside, the orange and white and blue paint on the buildings. The boats in the harbor, lined up and floating on the sparkling water. Seaplanes zipping in and out, a wall of greener than green trees, and the clouds scattering sunlight over the little town nestled into a hill.

Adelaide didn't step away from her spot until the ferry docked, only relenting to wheel her overstuffed suitcase onto land when ordered to by the loudspeaker voice.

She dragged the suitcase behind her, the wheels clacking over every bump. A young couple broke their embrace to rush around her. A fisherman clad in stained orange waders untied his boat, glancing at her.

He looked young to her – in his thirties, maybe? The same age her father had been when she'd thought he was so old and so wise, when he used to come home late and full of sighs. He used to shed his wet jacket at the door, the smell of fish and sea clinging to his skin as she jumped into his arms.

"Morning," the fisherman said, nodding at her.

It was rude to stare. Adelaide forced a smile. "Good morning."

She gripped the handle of her suitcase and kept walking.

She still couldn't stand to look at old pictures of her with her dad. It wasn't just because her father was gone, but because that girl was gone, too. The girl whose dreams she had betrayed.

"Aunt Addy!" a voice yelled.

She spun and spotted Mackenzie waving from the sidewalk.

Adelaide trotted over, grinning, and wrapped her into a hug. "It's so good to see you!"

Mackenzie held her close. "I can't believe you're really here!"

Adelaide pulled away, looking her up and down. "When did you turn into an adult?"

"Me, an adult?" Mackenzie stuck out her tongue. "I'm working on it. Granny is waiting in the car. Let me get your bag."

"I've got it," she said, but Mackenzie had already snatched it away.

She followed her to the car. Patty had the window down and jumped when Mackenzie opened the trunk.

"The radio is broken!" Patty said with a *tsk*. "I turned it up all the way and nothing is coming out."

Mackenzie leaned in and pressed a button. A song blasted through.

"Ah!" Patty yelled, swiping at the buttons. "Turn it off, turn it off!"

Mackenzie hit a button and the radio fell silent. "I think I found the problem. It was you."

"It was *not* me! This thing is too complicated!" Patty snapped. Her gaze settled on Adelaide and her eyes softened. "Adelaide! Welcome to San Juan Island! Hop in."

"Thank you so much for picking me up," she said, slipping into the backseat. "I promise not to cause any trouble."

"Ha!" Patty turned around to look at her. "I like a woman who causes some trouble. Trouble means someone is asking questions. Trouble means times are changing!"

"Trouble means a grandma getting into a fight with a radio," Mackenzie added.

Adelaide pushed her back into the seat, biting her lip, but Patty didn't argue. Instead, she threw her head back and laughed.

"The radio started it!"

Sheila had spent hours trying to convince Adelaide it would be okay for her to visit before Sheila returned from Europe, and in five minutes, Patty had proved her right.

Adelaide buckled her seat belt, her shoulders relaxing with each laughing breath.

"Now, Adelaide," Patty said as she pulled onto the street, "I wanted to keep you at my cottage, but Russell insisted you stay at his house."

"Oh, no, that's okay," she said. "I'm sure I can find a hotel somewhere."

"Don't even try it," Patty said. "The man has a five-bedroom house and it's wasting away. Well, Joey is there – his pilot – but he won't bother you. He's a nice boy."

Adelaide laughed. "I'm much more worried about me bothering him."

"He's hardly there," Mackenzie said. "He's always flying around."

"He's dating Eliza, isn't he?" Adelaide knew full well who Joey was. Sheila's calls had kept her afloat this last year after the divorce.

Nineteen years and, suddenly, silence.

"Yes. It really is a huge house," Mackenzie said. "Trust me, you're going to love it."

"Is it silly I feel like a student again, staying in hostels?" Adelaide paused. "Except I'm not a student anymore. Just an old divorced woman."

"You're a student of life," Patty corrected, pulling into a parking spot on the street. "Don't let yourself think any different. Now, is it all right with you if we pop into the grocery store for a second?"

"I don't mind."

They stepped onto the sidewalk. The heat wasn't oppressive here, and the wind was a mere cooling breeze. Strollers scooted by and a dog sniffed at her heel. A woman with a picnic basket walked arm-in-arm with a man, two children running ahead.

The island was alive. Nothing like the quiet of her apartment.

"How have you been holding up, dear?" Patty asked as they walked into the air-conditioned shop.

"Good. Very good," Adelaide said. There was no need to bore them with the truth.

An older woman pulled Patty aside, so Adelaide walked to the line of parked shopping carts with Mackenzie.

"I'm sorry about your divorce, Aunt Addy," Mackenzie said as she wrestled a cart out of the line.

"Oh, don't be sorry. I'm fine," Adelaide heard herself say. "Don't worry about me. I want to hear about *you*. You've got your whole life ahead of you!"

Mackenzie stopped the cart and looked her in the eye. Adelaide felt pressured to add the rest of her canned responses, but Mackenzie grabbed her by the arm.

"So do you. You deserve better than Uncle Shane."

She opened her mouth to respond, but a ball knotted her throat and tears pricked at her eyes. Normally, she'd have a joke at the ready to deflect, but she was fresh out of jokes.

One deep breath and she was able to speak. "That's sweet of you, Mackenzie."

"I love you, Aunt Addy." She patted her on the shoulder. "Sorry. Okay. Let's get some cheese. Do you want some cheese?"

"I'd love some cheese," she said with a laugh.

They were debating between a blueberry brie and a truffle camembert when Patty came over, clutching a paper in her hand. "It looks like we've got some trouble."

Mackenzie dropped the cheese. "Oh *no.*"

# Seventeen

**Initiative Measure 81823, The Protect Marine Mammals in Washington Initiative.** The proposed ordinance prohibits the buying, selling, or transportation of all marine mammals in the state of Washington. Should this Ordinance be enacted into law?

The air left Mackenzie's lungs. She forced a jagged breath and kept reading. "Vote yes in August on initiative 81823 to protect our marine mammals from exploitation."

She looked up at Granny. "What's this about? Capturing marine mammals is already illegal in this state. Why would someone propose this?"

"I think you know why." Granny sighed. "My friend Mary handed this flyer to me. She was excited. She thought it was something good."

"Wait," Adelaide said. "What's wrong with it?"

"If this goes into law, moving Lottie to the sea pen will be illegal," Mackenzie said. "It must have been Mrs. Smitt. I know it was."

"Oh. Wow." Adelaide stood, eyes wide. "Maybe they can make an exception?"

Mackenzie shook her head. "No way. This is targeted at us."

"It won't just hurt us, either," Granny said. "Think of the rescue team here on the island. They help stranded seals and porpoises all the time! They have to move them to rehabilitation for a few weeks before they're released. What are they supposed to do? Leave the poor things to roast in the sun?"

*Roast in the sun?* Mackenzie shuddered, staring at the flyer, the paper crinkling in her hand. "This is ridiculous."

"Sheila told me you're supposed to move Lottie soon," Adelaide said. "Could you get her here before this election?"

Mackenzie sighed. "No. We're waiting on the gate for the sea pen. It won't be delivered until the end of August – maybe even later."

"That Mrs. Smitt is one sneaky lady," Granny said, wagging a finger. "She must've submitted this months ago."

"Sneaky is too kind a word!" Mackenzie unwrinkled the paper and jabbed a finger at the top. "That wording is so misleading!"

"It is." Granny sighed. "If it could fool Mary, it could fool anyone."

"We need to get out of here," Mackenzie said, looking to the door. "We need to figure out a plan to fight this."

Granny laughed. "Now, hang on. I still need ice cream."

"There's no time for ice cream, Granny!" Mackenzie barked. "Let's go!"

Granny looked at Adelaide and smiled. "The world isn't going to go up in flames while I get my ice cream."

A laugh boomed out of Adelaide.

Mackenzie turned to her, mouth open. "Don't tell me you agree with her?"

"No, of course not. I agree with no one. I'm not involved!" Adelaide put her hands up, biting her lip, on the verge of laughing again.

Mackenzie rolled her eyes and smiled. This was the first glimmer of Aunt Addy's usual playfulness she'd seen. She'd allow Aunt Addy defying her if it meant she was feeling a bit better. "Fine. I will meet you two ice cream cones in the car."

"Ice cream cones?" Granny repeated, pushing the cart along. "Who knew ice cream cones could be used in a negative way?"

"Five minutes, Granny!" Mackenzie yelled, walking out the door.

. . .

Back in the car, Mackenzie got on her phone, searching. "I can't find out if Mrs. Smitt was the one who submitted this, but she had to be, right?"

"Does it matter?" Granny said, looking back at Adelaide. "I'll take you to Russell's house first, dear. You can get settled and, when you're ready, we've got a tea party planned for you."

A smile spread across Adelaide's face. "A tea party? For me?"

"Of course! You're our guest of honor!"

Mackenzie looked over her shoulder. Her aunt's cheeks were pink.

"You're going to like it," she said before turning back to her phone.

"That's very kind of you. Thank you."

They got to Russell's and Mackenzie excused herself to run up the hill and into the tea shop.

"Eliza!" She yelled. "I have terrible news!"

Liam was there, his elbow on the front counter, a bemused smile on his face. "Are the boaters back?"

She stopped. "Oh. Hi, Liam." She shoved the flyer into his hand. "Look at this! It has to be Mrs. Smitt's doing. She's trying to stop us from moving Lottie."

His eyes scanned, and creases formed on his forehead. "Don't you think people will see through this?"

"Why would they? It sounds like voting *no* means you hate dolphins."

"I thought I heard yelling," Eliza said, walking out of the kitchen. "Hey, Mack."

Liam handed her the flyer. "Apparently there's going to be a special election in a few weeks."

"Yeah, and Lottie will end up grounded for who knows how long," Mackenzie said. "I can't believe Mrs. Smitt came up with this. I underestimated her. I'm going to fly over there and toss her into that tank. We'll see how she likes it!"

Eliza winced, carefully folding the flyer in half. "Mackenzie, please do not throw anyone into a whale tank because you are upset with them."

"Oh, come on. Lottie wouldn't hurt her. What I meant is, how would she like living in a little fishbowl for the rest of her life?"

"I think we should let Mackenzie do what needs to be done," Liam said with a shrug. "I, for one, would like to see if Smitt can swim."

Eliza rolled her eyes. "Where's Aunt Addy? Did you forget her at the ferry landing?"

"No." Mackenzie sighed. "She's here. She's fine. Granny's setting her up at Russell's, then they're coming for the tea party. But we don't have time for that right now."

Eliza crossed her arms over her chest. "Are you going to tell Granny that?"

"Obviously not." She sat on a chair. The wooden legs shrieked across the floor. "I can't cross Granny. She's too dangerous."

"We just need to explain to people what this measure means," Liam said. "Then they'll understand, and they'll vote no."

Her stomach felt heavy, like it was full of seawater. She looked up at him. "What if they don't want Lottie to be moved? Some people think we're just going to dump her in the ocean to fend for herself. They think we're trying to kill her – but we're not! She's going to have a great retirement in a beautiful, huge sea pen where she's safe and protected. She's still going to be taken care of, and she might even get to see her mom again."

"If I didn't know the whole story, it *would* sort of sound like the ranting of a mad woman," Eliza said, cracking a smile.

Mackenzie narrowed her eyes. "Are you serious right now? Do you want me to throw you in the tank, too?"

She put her hands up. "I'm just kidding! I was trying to lighten the mood."

"What if," Liam said, clearing his throat, "we talk to some people? Go door to door, explain why the measure doesn't make sense. See what they're thinking. A poll, of sorts."

"We can't go to every door in the state before August," Mackenzie said.

"No, but we can get a feel for what people think about the issue. If the circumstances behind the measure are explained, they might change their minds."

Mackenzie sat, staring at the floor. She could see Mrs. Smitt's smarmy face in her mind's eye. Her anger bubbled like lava. The skin on her chest and arms glowed red.

If Mrs. Smitt ever dared to set foot on San Juan Island, Mackenzie would have her arrested.

"Mackenzie?" Liam asked.

She looked up. "Yes?"

"What do you think about the poll? After we get an idea of what people are thinking, we can make something about the measure and how it relates to Lottie. Mail it out, maybe."

"This is a great idea," Eliza said, nodding.

The chair was digging into her back. She stood. "We don't have time."

"We have plenty of time," he said calmly. "We can start now."

"Right now?" She bit her lip. She wanted Joey to fly her to the mainland. It shouldn't be too hard to find where Mrs. Smitt lived. She could set up a speaker outside her window to blare banjo music twenty-four hours a day...

"You can satisfy your bloodlust another time," Liam said, a half smile on his face. "For now, let's make sure we can get Lottie into the sea pen as soon as it's ready."

Mackenzie unclenched her jaw. "Fine. I'll get my computer. We'll make a fact sheet."

"Great."

She paused on her way to the back door. "Are you sure you don't want to pay Mrs. Smitt a visit first?"

He raised an eyebrow. "We can crank call her, but that should be the extent of our contact."

"Fine." Crank calls were a good start. She smiled, her skin cooling, the lava hardening a path ahead. "I'll take it."

# Eighteen

Their Lottie flyer came together seamlessly. Liam sat, watching Mackenzie as she worked, feeling as useless as the spare chair at their table.

She clicked away, pausing only to bite at her nails, conducting a symphony only she could hear.

Within half an hour, she ran back to the cottage to print copies, leaving Liam sitting there, stunned.

"I don't know if I've been much help," Liam said.

Eliza set a teapot on the table next to him. "You've been a huge help. You're a calming force. Mackenzie needs that. Without you, she might've committed a crime by now."

He laughed. "She wouldn't."

Eliza raised her eyebrows.

"Would she?" he asked.

The front door jingled open and Patty walked in, followed by a slight woman with brown hair and Mackenzie's gray eyes.

"Aunt Addy!" Eliza ran over, colliding into a hug.

"Eliza!" Addy said. "It's beautiful in here! Patty told me what you've done with the place."

"I've just been helping out," she said with a shrug.

Patty waved a hand. "Nonsense. You brought my tea shop back to life."

Should he get up? Excuse himself? Liam didn't need to be part of this family reunion, but he couldn't stop staring at Adelaide. The family resemblance was jarring.

"Your table is set, ladies." Eliza waved a hand. "Mackenzie should be joining us as soon as she's finished with her rampage."

Patty chuckled.

Liam tore his eyes away and stood from his seat. "I should be going. I don't want to impose on your tea party."

"What is that!" Patty gasped, pointing over his shoulder.

He turned around. It was just the painting he'd made of the tea shop – the one *without* Mackenzie's figure against the sea. That version was safely tucked away in his room.

"It's a gift," Liam said. "Eliza thought you might like it."

She walked over to the canvas, lifting it up with both hands. "Liam! This is gorgeous. You are so talented. Russell knows how to pick his friends."

He looked away. "Ha, right. Enjoy your tea."

She grabbed him by the arm. "Adelaide, this is Russell's artist in residence, Liam."

He nodded. "Nice to meet you."

"That painting is really lovely," Adelaide said, looking up at him with Mackenzie's eyes.

"Thank you." He took another step toward the door. "I should probably get back to—"

The front door flung open and Mackenzie pushed through. "Okay, I printed fifty copies. Do you think we can do fifty houses today?" she asked, then stopped. "Wow, Granny. Where'd you get that painting?"

"Liam gave it to me." She held the canvas up, beaming. "Isn't it beautiful?"

She tilted her head ever so slightly. "It is."

Eliza covered her mouth, laughing. "It was sitting next to you the whole time you were working and you didn't notice it."

Mackenzie winced. "Oops."

Liam reached for the flyers, gently taking them from her hand. "Mackenzie, why don't you enjoy tea with your family and I'll get started on polling people."

Her brow furrowed. In this light, her eyes were slightly more green than her aunt's. As variable and mysterious as the sea...

"Are you sure?" she asked.

He nodded. "I'll report back soon. I think you'll be relieved at the results."

"Make sure you use all the talking points I wrote out," she said. "If they have any questions, they should ask me. Maybe name drop Russell if things aren't going well."

"Noted." He smiled. "Enjoy your tea."

He reached the door and Mackenzie spoke again. "Sorry I missed your painting earlier. It's stunning."

"Oh, thanks. It's nothing special, but I'm glad your granny likes it."

"No, it's really beautiful. I think I'm just blind to beauty right now." She smiled and shrugged. "Sorry."

He was staring again. He looked down. "You're on a mission. It's understandable." Liam turned to the door. "I'll talk to you soon."

"Thank you! And good luck!"

# Nineteen

The tea party with Aunt Addy was fine, but the longer it dragged on, the more antsy Mackenzie grew.

After Liam left, Granny's boyfriend Reggie stopped by, his eyes bright and his arms full of wildflowers.

"Sorry I'm late," he said as he sat down. "I couldn't come empty handed, and when I picked these up, I got into a half hour chat about the pair of kayakers getting pulled out to sea."

"Oh no! Are they okay?" Addy asked.

"Thankfully, yes. You can never be too careful with the ocean. It has a mind of its own," Reggie said.

"I'm glad you're here." Eliza sprung from her seat. "I'll get you some soup."

More soup. *Great.*

Mackenzie held her groan in, boring her stare into the ceiling. Leave it up to Eliza to find a bunch of soup recipes and start the long process of perfecting them. Now they were stuck eating soup at a tea party.

What kind of tea party had soup anyway?

Aunt Addy wasn't complaining, though, and she was the guest of honor. Come to think of it, she wasn't talking much at all.

She seemed engaged, though. She laughed a lot. When Eliza did an impression of their mom making excuses for not finishing her newest music album, Aunt Addy was in stitches, wiping tears from her eyes.

Still, she didn't seem totally herself. Her spark was missing.

Oh, how Mackenzie hated Uncle Shane for snuffing out that spark. She'd never particularly liked him, but she loved Aunt Addy so much it didn't matter.

Mackenzie could tell her anything. When they were little, Aunt Addy was always the one to play dress up and hide and seek and jump into the pool. She didn't care about getting her hair wet or looking silly. Sometimes, it felt like she was just a much older sister.

How was Aunt Addy getting through this divorce? Maybe she could teach Mackenzie a thing or two.

So far, Mackenzie's best technique for getting through her own breakup had been to keep busy – and to daydream. She'd managed to block most of her sad flashbacks by replacing them with visions of success: a star-studded Blackfish Ball, Lottie leaping with joy in the ocean, and maybe, just *maybe*, a news story with a picture of her face floating its way back to her ex, Steve.

Was it conceited to want him to see what she was doing? Maybe. But it was how she was getting by, particularly after pictures from his engagement party had flooded every corner of her phone.

She couldn't stop looking at them, and when she wasn't looking at them, she was thinking about them. Where did his fiancée get her dress? Who were all those people at the party? Why did they hire a DJ? What kind of people needed an ice sculpture of a giant heart at their engagement party?

Deep down, she knew Steve's impending blissful marriage wasn't her problem. *She* was her problem.

Whether she'd admit it out loud or not, Mackenzie knew some teeny, tiny vain part of her was determined to rescue Russell's mess so she could throw it in Steve's face.

Mackenzie couldn't help it. She needed to *win*, and the risk of it all blowing up in her face kept her going.

What if she failed Lottie? What if they couldn't get the sea pen built or if Mrs. Smitt got her way? What if the amazing job at Opuluxe Escapes got snatched away as soon as Cameron realized what a fraud she was and she never got another job in sales again?

Her stomach lurched and she pushed her bowl away. That was enough soup for today.

She needed to get back to what she could control. She pulled out her phone and texted Liam.

**How's it going?**

It took fifteen minutes to get a reply.

**Not bad. I made it four houses before a lady insisted I come in for milk and cookies.**

Mackenzie stifled a laugh. **Don't tell me you went inside.**

**I did. It's been over an hour. I've helped her hang a curtain rod and three pictures of her grandkids.**

She burst out laughing.

"What's so funny?" Eliza asked, gathering empty bowls. "Is my soup bad? Are you texting Shelby and Emma about it?"

Mackenzie set her phone down. "No, Eliza, I don't have a secret text group with our sisters to make fun of your soup."

Eliza stared, biting her lip.

"The soup was great!" Mackenzie insisted. "I'm laughing because I just got a text from Liam. A sweet old lady lured him into her home with milk and cookies. I think I need to rescue him."

Eliza laughed. "Fine, but hurry back. I made mini lemon pudding cakes."

"Wouldn't miss it for the world." She got up from the table and stepped outside to make the call.

He answered quickly. "Hello?"

"Hello, dear. Are you coming home?"

A slight pause, then, "Oh. Yes. I'll be home soon. So sorry."

"Hurry up, Liam!" she yelled. "I've been waiting an hour!"

A laugh snorted out of her and she quickly ended the call, returning to her seat.

His message came five minutes later.

**Thanks for that. She finally released me, though she made me promise to come back tomorrow to fix a running toilet.**

**I hope the cookies were worth it**, she wrote back.

She watched the dots on her screen as he typed his response.

**Saved you one to judge for yourself.**

She smiled. That was nice of him.

**I'm sorry, but I don't know if I'll be able to join you today. We're having the longest tea party ever and Granny's insisting we have a fire on the beach afterward. You should probably keep the cookie for yourself.**

He wrote back quickly.

**No problem at all. I'll keep going. I'm happy to help, and excited about my budding handyman business.**

"Mackenzie!" Eliza barked.

Her head shot up. "Sorry. What did I miss?"

She put her hands on her hips. "My lemon pudding cakes. Do you want one?"

"Yes, they look great. Thank you." Mackenzie grabbed a cake and tucked her phone away. She had to trust Liam to handle the polling on his own. As much as it killed her to stand by idly, she didn't have much of a choice at the moment.

# Twenty

The last splashes of orange faded into the sunset. Liam returned to find Mackenzie and crew on the beach trying—and failing—to set up a bonfire.

"You're welcome to stay," Patty shouted as she set out marshmallows, chocolate bars, and graham crackers. Her golden retriever Derby stood a foot behind her, staring at the marshmallows. "You could use those big strong arms of yours to carry some firewood!"

"I think Liam's done enough for us today," Mackenzie said. She turned back to him. "I hope you're not super tired."

"Not at all. I made it to twenty-two houses, and fifteen people were willing to talk." He held up a clear plastic bag with a chocolate chip cookie inside. "And one, as you know, tricked me with baked goods."

Mackenzie laughed. She accepted the cookie and took a bite, the chocolate chunk snapping in her teeth. "I can see why you stayed so long. This is a good cookie."

He liked seeing her in this light. She looked more relaxed with her family. Even their arguments were lighthearted, like the tone in her voice when she'd called him with the "Hello dear..."

How his heart had leapt at those words.

"I know it doesn't seem like I did much today," he said, "but the results were consistent. Every single person initially said they would vote yes on the initiative, but when I handed them the flyer and explained a few things, they changed their minds."

Mackenzie finished off the rest of the cookie. "I guess that's half good news."

"It's fully good news. One of the women I spoke to used to volunteer for local elections. She said we could send these flyers out as political mail if we work with the post office. I was thinking we could add a picture of Lottie, simplify some of the language, then send them out."

"Yes, of course. Why didn't I think of that?" She shook her head. "We'll start with the islands, then make adjustments before we send them to every voter in the state of Washington."

He nodded. "Right."

"We can go to the post office tomorrow. I think we can find a printer to make sure the flyer is in color..."

Patty walked over, a stack of newspapers in her arms. "Excuse me, young lady. Tomorrow we're meeting with Margie at Saltwater Cove," she said. "Don't you remember? You're going over the details for the ball, and you're bringing me with you. I have to return Margie's cake box."

Mackenzie groaned. "I forgot. Russell really needs to give me a raise or hire a real project manager."

"I'll go to the post office," Liam said. "I don't mind."

She eyed him. "Are you sure?"

"Consider it done."

She stepped back, looking at him. "Oh. Thanks, Liam."

Eliza joined them, wiping her forehead and leaving a black smudge on her brow. "I'm done with fire management. We're not having a fire. Everyone can go home and go to sleep."

Liam smiled. "Mind if I try?"

She handed him a lighter and a roll of newspaper. "Knock yourself out."

"You should tell Russell you're moving into one of his spare bedrooms, Liam," Patty said. "You deserve a raise, too! You shouldn't be stuck on that faraway island."

He squatted beside the fire pit. Bits of charred newspaper scattered as he picked up a log. "I like it on Stuart. I like the peace. Though the company is better here."

"The boater bros kind of ruin the peace, don't they?" Mackenzie asked, looking down on him with her arms crossed.

That wasn't what he'd meant. He smiled at her. "A bit."

Mackenzie laughed and he tore his eyes away, turning back to the fire. He shifted the logs into a standing teepee, tossing aside two waterlogged branches, and stuffed a bundle of newspaper inside.

With a snap of the lighter, the newspaper caught fire for a moment, then vanished in the wind. Liam lit it again and again, shielding the little flame with his hands, until it licked the nearest twigs, spreading steadily. Within a minute, the entire structure crackled, engulfed in flames.

He stood and Patty clapped him on the shoulder. "Is there anything you can't do?"

"Oh, lots." Liam looked up. "Like fly a plane."

Joey, his mouth full of graham crackers, walked over. "That's my cue."

"Oh, hey man. I don't mean to rush you."

"No rush. I'm on track to eat all the chocolate before anyone can roast a marshmallow."

"Cut that out!" Mackenzie barked. "You're going to make the s'mores uneven!"

"There's no such thing as uneven s'mores!" Eliza shouted, kneeling by the fire. "Leave Joey alone!"

"Children," Patty said, "there are plenty of supplies for everyone."

Joey laughed. "I'll take you back. Follow me."

Liam turned to follow Joey down the hill. Halfway there, Joey paused.

"Do you mind if I run to the house real quick? I need to grab something."

"No problem."

Joey walked on and Liam stood, hanging in the darkness, the smell of rich smoke riding the cool night air.

Darkness fell astonishingly quickly, surrounding him like a heavy blanket. He took a few steps back up the hill until he could see the warm glow of the flames.

Eliza knelt beside the fire, loading marshmallows onto a roasting fork. "You're holding your fork too high, Aunt Addy," she said, shaking her head. "You're going to be here forever."

Mackenzie walked over and thrust a roasting fork directly into the fire.

Flames danced around the edges before catching, turning it into a beacon. She waved it wildly above her head until the flames went out.

"That's the wrong way to toast a marshmallow!" Eliza snapped. "It'll end up cold at the center and burnt on the outside."

Mackenzie stepped away, eyeing her blackened marshmallow. "I'll just wait for you to make me one, then."

Liam smiled to himself. He wouldn't have expected Mackenzie to roast a marshmallow any other way.

Mackenzie dropped her fork on the ground and knelt next to Derby. His head was bowed, his mouth slightly open.

"Derby!" she hissed, prying his jaws open with both hands. Wet marshmallows fell out of his mouth. She gathered them and stood. "You are too old to be getting into stuff like this."

He wagged his tail, head hanging low.

Liam stifled a laugh and Mackenzie looked up, catching him standing in the darkness.

She jumped. "Is everything okay?"

He sucked in a breath. "Oh, yes, sorry. Joey had to stop by the house, so I thought I'd keep warm here."

"Do you want a s'more?" she asked, dumping the stolen marshmallows into the flames.

She looked so pretty, the flames dancing in her eyes. He didn't want anything except to stay here for the rest of the night with her.

Except he couldn't form the words. "No, but thanks. I'd better get going."

# Twenty-one

"Oh. Okay." Mackenzie hesitated. If it wasn't s'mores he wanted, then what was it?

Liam nodded, flashed a brief smile, and turned.

Mackenzie watched him disappear. She squinted into the darkness, seeing only a few twinkling lights.

A flutter rose in her chest. Something didn't feel right. She wasn't sure what, but something was off.

"Mackenzie! Do you want two chocolate bars on yours, or just one?" Eliza called out.

"I thought Joey ate them all?" she yelled back, grinning.

The uneasy feeling dissipated as she turned back around, fading into her memory like a bit of floating ash.

The next morning, Mackenzie got up early to prepare for Saltwater Cove. Granny had insisted on tagging along, even though Mackenzie was perfectly capable of dropping off a cake box.

"I like to return things in person," Granny said. "Plus, Hank has an apple tree he's grafting that I wanted to see. Don't worry. I'll stay out of the way."

"You don't have to explain anything to me, Granny," Mackenzie said, keeping her eyes forward. They were on a particularly beautiful stretch of road, the farmland spanning either side. A line of bicyclists rode ahead, setting the pace. "I know you're just coming to look for signs that Idris Elba will be at the ball."

She giggled and waved a hand. "Oh stop! You're wicked."

Poor Granny, always holding out hope for her Hollywood crush. If he were coming, Margie would know, and she would've already spilled the beans. They'd been friends for years – almost as soon as Margie had landed on the island.

Mackenzie knew Margie's story by heart at this point. Granny told everyone how Margie had moved to the island after her divorce and bought her brother's house for a dollar. How she'd single-handedly turned the barn into a popular wedding venue and charmed Hank, the broody Chief Deputy Sheriff, into marrying her.

Granny liked to finish her retelling with, "Theirs is a *real* love story."

Mackenzie had only gotten to know Chief Hank recently, but she liked him immensely. He'd flat out refused to arrest Eliza when all that bank robbery nonsense was going on, and his cool-headed help was always available when she needed it.

She didn't know Margie as well. She seemed nice, but Mackenzie doubted *nice* would be enough to escape the curse Russell had left them.

Still. It was best to keep that to herself.

When they pulled up to the barn at Saltwater Cove, Margie was waiting outside. "Hello, hello, hello!"

Her pink dress flowed in the breeze, skirting over a pair of muddy yellow rain boots.

Mackenzie parked the car and got out. "Hi, Margie."

"Mackenzie! Welcome!" She hugged her, then moved on to Granny. "You didn't have to bring that old cake box back. It's not worth the trouble."

"I'm here for support," Granny said with a wink.

Mackenzie raised an eyebrow. "You're here to be nosy."

Granny stuck out her lip. "I've never been nosy in my life."

"Please excuse my muddy boots," Margie said, wiping her brow. A pile of dark earth lay at her feet, the flowerbeds dug up and disrupted. "I'm sneaking in a few more flowers before the event. I want to make sure everything is perfect for the Blackfish Ball. I love what you're doing for Lottie."

Mackenzie let out a breath. "Thank you. I'm just trying to get everyone through this in one piece."

Margie waved a hand. "Oh stop. It's going to be grand. You'll see!"

"I'm going to find that husband of yours," Granny said, walking toward the house.

"Be good, Patty!" Margie turned to Mackenzie. "Though I know she never is."

"No, she really isn't." Mackenzie cracked a smile. "It's beautiful here."

"Thanks. We try." Margie started walking. "Patty mentioned you wanted to add some people to the guest list?"

Mackenzie made a face, sucking air through her teeth. "Yes, but I don't know how it's going to work. There are almost a hundred more people who want to attend. We're already at the two-fifty max, but I don't know how to tell someone *no* when they offer to make a donation."

"Well, that's easy. Don't tell them no!" Margie said with a laugh. "Take their check and tell them to come on over. Don't worry about space. Last year we had a wedding with almost four hundred people. We have two hundred and fifty seats for dinner, but we can add more seats under the tent. Or make it standing room only and fit in even more."

"So we could make some people VIPs?" Mackenzie asked. "And some non-VIPs. Maybe stick my family under the tent."

"Sure. That will be easy."

Her chest was stiff from holding a tense breath. She let it out. "I'm always worried about running out of food, too."

"Don't be. I can get enough to feed an army. Besides, most people don't eat for long. They want to dance and mingle and be gazed upon."

Orange poppies were growing in bunches along the barn. She loved the poppies, their burst of life in the grass. The muscles in Mackenzie's shoulders softened. "That sounds about right."

"Let me show you the barn."

Margie pulled the massive doors open and they walked inside. Strings of bistro lights hung from rafter to rafter, and shining wooden tables stretched the length of the room.

"Normally, I like to keep the dinner seating in here and have music outside. You hired a live band, right?"

"Yes. Dukes and Dahlias. I'm hoping they show up."

"They'll show." She nodded. "We work with them all the time. I'll set them up just outside under the tent. That way, people can still hear the music when they escape into here for a bite to eat. At night, we turn on these fairy lights to lead the way."

Fairy lights? "That sounds magical."

"I was thinking of hanging some banners here," Margie continued, both hands suspended in the air, "with pictures of Lottie. One could be from where she was captured, one from her little tank at the park, and one picture of the sea pen. What do you think?"

Mackenzie stood with her hands on her hips, squinting at the bare wall. "I think you have better ideas for this thing than I do. I'm just going to let you run with it."

Margie clapped her hands together. "Wonderful! I was hoping you'd say that. I'll have the banners made; don't worry about that. Did you get a chance to look at the caterer list?"

Mackenzie nodded. "Your recommendations seemed perfect."

"Good. Now, for the photography, we have a dear family friend named Morgan who said she'd love to work the event for free."

"Oh, wow. That's perfect!"

"I know some of the famous people insisted on there being no cameras inside, so we'll set up a red carpet and let her snap away!"

They walked around the property for the next hour, surveying the tents, tables, and finally the cove after which the barn was named.

"We get stunning sunsets here, and the view under the starlight is mesmerizing," Margie said, standing on the rocky beach. "I know your guests are going to be dressed up, so we'll put out our portable flooring to make a path to the cove. That way, anyone wearing high heels won't sink into the beach."

"You've really thought of everything," Mackenzie said, staring out at the water. It was a deep, calming blue.

"It does get cooler in the evenings," Margie went on, "so we'll bring out the electric fire pits. We have lounges and chairs, and I always put out blankets."

Mackenzie couldn't stop herself from laughing. "I feel silly for even coming here. You're clearly the boss of this ball."

Margie grinned. "I'm just glad you're happy with it. If you think of anything else, please let me know." She gasped. "Oh, would you want hot chocolate and cookies to go for the guests as they leave? The cookies would be black and white and shaped like little killer whales. Is that okay?"

Mackenzie snorted a laugh. "That is more than okay, Margie."

"Good." She grinned and took a deep breath. "I think this will be the event of the season."

The photographer was a nice touch. Mackenzie hadn't even thought of that. Who knew? Maybe some of these pictures would end up in front of Steve, and he'd see the glitz and glamour, and he'd see Cameron at her side...

Not that it was the point, but it would be nice.

Mackenzie smiled. This was the first time she'd allowed herself to feel any excitement about the ball. "I can't wait to see this come together."

# Twenty-two

C hatting with Hank was always a delight. Patty loved the gossip from the sheriff's department, particularly when she got to pry it out of Hank.

"So you're telling me you have *no* idea who donated the money for the new K9?"

"Nope," Hank said, a smile creeping to his eyes. "And if I did, I wouldn't tell you."

Patty sat at the little kitchen table in their house, tea in hand, her shoulders shaking with laughter. "You're a menace, Hank. Did you know that?"

The door opened and Mackenzie peeked in. "Hey, Granny. I'm all set. Are you ready to go?"

She sighed, bracing her hand on the table to stand. "I suppose so. Hank is tired of my questioning."

"Not at all," he said, getting up from his seat. "I'm just glad you took off the wires for the lie detector test."

Mackenzie's eyes darted between them. "Granny, you can't keep bringing your lie detector to people's homes."

"Aha, but I have it with me everywhere I go." She tapped a finger to her forehead. "Hank, thank you for the tea. We'll be seeing you again soon."

"Am I invited to the elite Blackfish Ball?" he asked, eyebrows raised.

"Of course!" Patty said. "You live here, and you double as security. Not to mention I owe you one for helping Eliza."

"You told me you'd gut me like a fish if I arrested her."

Patty scoffed. "I would never say something like that."

She walked out, gave Margie a hug goodbye, and loaded herself into the car.

"I don't think you're supposed to threaten a sheriff, Granny," Mackenzie said as they pulled onto the road.

"I said if he was cowardly enough to arrest my granddaughter, I'd gut him like the yellowtail he was," Patty said. "That's not a threat. It's a fact."

Mackenzie flashed a look at her, eyebrows strung together. "That's even worse! That's, like, creative!"

She shrugged. "I've always told you, Mackenzie. If you need to make a statement, you might as well make it memorable. But don't be vulgar. They'll only use that against you."

"You've literally never said that."

Patty paused, combing through her memories. It was all fuzzy. There were too many of them. "Well, I meant to say it. Maybe you should write it down."

She laughed. "I'll get on that."

Patty settled back into her seat. Mackenzie's car had a much smoother ride than her own. Maybe she should consider upgrading? Then again, what a waste it would be, a new car. Hers was fine for driving from one side of the island to the other. "How do things look for the ball?"

"To tell you the truth, I'm more concerned than ever."

Patty turned to look at her. "What!"

"It seems too perfect." Mackenzie shook her head. "Something is bound to go wrong."

"Oh." Patty laughed. "Have some faith. You have more friends than you know."

Mackenzie scoffed. "Yeah, right. Russell ran off to Europe with Mom and left me here to deal with the contractors and drunken boaters and angry old ladies."

"I'm not angry. I'm feisty. There's a difference."

"Not you," she said, rolling her eyes. "Mrs. Smitt."

Patty looked back out the window. "Believe it or not, I remember being your age. I remember the intense emotions and ideas of youth."

"Granny, this isn't me being intense. This *is* intense!"

"Sure, sure."

Mackenzie sighed. "Am I really about to get a lecture because I'm trying my best?"

"Not a lecture." She reached over and patted her hand. "I think you might need to stop and take a deep breath. Maybe adjust your attitude."

"I always need to adjust my attitude," Mackenzie said. "Especially when things keep going wrong in ways I never expected."

"You found friends you never expected, didn't you?"

Mackenzie shrugged.

Patty went on. "Don't turn your nose up at help! Look at Margie. She's an ally. She's a helper."

"She is. I'll give you that."

She stared at Mackenzie. Her mouth was twisted, like she was chronically in pain.

"I can't tell you everything is going to be okay," Patty said. "No one can. What I *can* tell you is, no matter what, you will be okay. You have the strength, you have the resilience. Believe in yourself."

Mackenzie stared straight forward, eyes on the road a thousand miles ahead.

"And believe in your friends," Patty added. "It's not just Margie."

"Eliza?"

"Well, yes, of course."

She cocked her head. "You?"

Was Mackenzie really *that* blind? How funny, to be so young, so intensely focused on the wrong things. "That goes without saying, but you've made new friends recently."

Mackenzie tapped her hand on the steering wheel. "Liam?"

It was hard not to laugh. How had it taken her so long to realize who she was talking about? "Yes, Liam! He doesn't have to help you, you know, but he does anyway. And you're not particularly nice to him."

"I know." She laughed. "He's an odd one."

Patty clenched her hands together. That wasn't what she was getting at. Patty had seen Liam's type before, and she would bet her imaginary new car he was someone Mackenzie could count on.

*Should* count on.

His eyes were full of love, full of affection, but he didn't say a word, instead keeping it locked in his heart like the ever-burning flame of a lighthouse.

He wasn't odd at all. Just, unfortunately, rare.

"I like him," Patty finally said.

"Should we stop at the bakery on the way home?" Mackenzie asked, flipping on her turn signal.

Patty sighed. Mackenzie couldn't see it yet. Hopefully she wouldn't wait until it was too late. "Of course. I never say no to a bakery."

# Twenty-three

The last thing Mackenzie needed was another distraction. The Blackfish Ball was in less than two weeks, and she had a hundred details to chase down before the guests arrived.

Her mom and Russell were scheduled to fly in the morning of the ball, and above all else, she was determined to show Russell she'd handled the mess he'd left her with grace and ease.

She was locked away in her room, tallying the last-minute dietary requests on a notepad, when her phone rang.

"If it's not the caterers, I'm not answering," she muttered, glancing over.

She did a double take. Cameron.

Mackenzie snatched the phone to her ear. "Hello?"

"Hey! How are you doing?"

She dropped her pen and sat up. "Good. I'm finalizing a few details for the ball. Nothing major. How are you?"

"Ah, I can't wait. It's been too long since I've been to a good ball."

She laughed. "I didn't take you for a ball enthusiast."

"You don't have me pegged, Mackenzie."

A flutter hit her stomach. *Clearly.* "I'm so sorry. My apologies. I should've consulted you sooner."

"You should have." He laughed and cleared his throat. "I'm headed to the island now for business, but I saw the dance studio in town has tango lessons tonight. I was hoping I'd see you there."

Mackenzie laughed. "Dance lessons?"

The last thing in the world she had time for was tango lessons.

"You probably don't need lessons; you're so good at everything," he sighed. "I'm not so lucky. I'll be there. All alone. No partner or anything."

She looked down at her desk and the scribbles on her notepad. The checklist of to-do's was as long as her arm, with a second list spanning another page.

She needed to double check ferry reservations for the band. There was a problem with the hydrangea order and she had to decide if the upcharge for viburnum was worth it. The guy she'd rented a red carpet from had disappeared from the face of the earth, and the caricature artist had hinted *again* about needing five-star accommodations to do her best work.

"Unless," he added, "you decide to join me?"

She grinned down at her desk. Her heartbeat thudded in her ears. "Is this an official Opuluxe Escapes event?"

"It's whatever you want it to be."

Her heart leapt.

"Okay," she heard herself say. "I'll be there."

"Great. I'll send you the details."

She hung up the call and sat at her desk, her limbs tingling. *Whatever you want it to be.* What was that supposed to mean?

Was he still trying to get her to work for Opuluxe Escapes? Or was this...something else?

A text popped up with the time and place. She only had four hours until the class started.

Mackenzie took a deep breath and turned back to her checklist, her eyes snapping into focus. She looked at the top of her list: Flower order mix-up.

She dialed the number of the florist. "Hi, yeah. The carnations are fine. Thank you."

Done. Next up, the ferry. She had no idea what her password or username was for the online system, which had put her off dealing with this. There was no time to dillydally now. She reset it, checked the reservation was for the correct time and date, and sent a confirmation to the band.

Done.

An hour before the tango class, Mackenzie had accomplished everything she needed for the day, plus a few tasks she didn't think she'd get to until tomorrow. It was amazing what a goal could do to her productivity.

She stood from her desk and walked to the mirror. Should she wear her hair up? Add more makeup or act like she didn't care?

The fact that she was even thinking about it meant she cared. *Whatever you want it to be.*

Her heart jumped into her throat. What did she want it to be?

Mackenzie shook her head and picked up her makeup bag. Fresh mascara and a dab of lipstick never hurt. She changed into a black sheath dress and stared at herself in the mirror. It didn't look too try-hard. She could be running to the store or going to a work meeting.

Or going on her first date with her future husband.

Only kidding. She turned away from the mirror. She didn't believe that, not really. But it wasn't impossible.

She'd wasted so much time with Steve. What if Cameron was the one she was supposed to end up with? The other half of her power couple, the one she'd been looking for? What if she'd been after the wrong salesman all along?

Her family loved to tease her for missing things right in front of her face. Being able to focus – being able to see a *win* so clearly – was useful, but it gave her tunnel vision at times. She could admit that.

Dancing needed heels, right? She'd read that somewhere. She bent down, rummaging through the shoe rack at the foot of her bed until her hand landed on the smooth black leather on her favorite pair of heels.

She hadn't worn them in months. They'd help with the dancing – help her stay on the balls of her feet. And if they made her legs look long and graceful? That was an unavoidable side effect.

Mackenzie slipped on the shoes, crept down the stairs, and got to her car completely unnoticed. She wasn't hiding anything, but it was best to avoid having to explain herself to Granny and Eliza. She didn't know what she would've said.

Did she even *want* to work at Opuluxe Escapes? Sure, she might be able to make a bunch of money and rise to the top of the sales department. She could recreate herself and prove to herself – and Steve – she didn't need any of them to succeed.

Somehow, none of that seemed as exciting as the tone of Cameron's voice, the glint in his caramel eyes, the touch of his hand on her waist...

Her chest fluttered. She wasn't doing that again. No dating coworkers. She'd learned her lesson.

But she could always work somewhere else. Then the coworker thing would be a nonissue.

Mackenzie put her hands on the steering wheel and drove to the studio. There was a parking spot directly outside and she pulled in, staring through the windows.

Ballet bars ran along all three walls, each covered in full-length mirrors. The polished wood floor shone under recessed lights. A svelte woman in a belly shirt strutted around, smiling and greeting the four couples gathered near the front.

Cameron stood near the door, the sleeves to his blue button up shirt rolled up, exposing the rippled muscles on his forearms.

Mackenzie sucked in a breath. Maybe she shouldn't have come. Maybe she wasn't ready for anything new. She could make an excuse, tell him she was busy.

At that moment, he turned and caught her eye. He smiled. Waved.

She raised a hand and waved back.

Too late now.

He opened the door as she approached. "I'm so glad you came." He dropped his voice low. "I didn't realize this class catered to an *older* crowd."

As though that was her primary concern.

"You'll find we have a robust retiree community here on the island," Mackenzie said. "Which is lucky, because they like tea."

"That is helpful for a tea shop, isn't it?"

How long was this going to take? Maybe they could grab dinner after. Mackenzie scanned the room, looking for a poster or a sign, when she spotted a woman's smiling face.

"You're Patty's granddaughter, aren't you?" She pointed, walking over.

Mackenzie nodded. "One of them. Yes."

"Hear me out," she said, putting an arm on Mackenzie's shoulder. "I know about the ball and I think you lost my invitation."

Mackenzie let out a slow breath. "Did I?"

"Yes. Patty swears up and down she has no control over it, but you must. I'm a great dancer. I've got the moves. I'll class it up." She grinned and raised her eyebrows.

"If you're such a great dancer," Cameron said, "why are you in this beginner's class?"

A scowl swirled onto her face. "Oh, a comedian. Don't tell me *you're* invited and I'm not!"

He nodded. "I'm the entertainment."

She narrowed her eyes. "I've been a member of this community for twenty-three years and—"

The teacher in the belly shirt clapped her hands together. "All right, everyone! Please bring yourselves close. Our lesson is about to begin!"

The woman cast one last look at Cameron before walking back to her partner.

"Thanks for the backup," Mackenzie muttered. "I can't go anywhere with Granny without someone trying to get an invitation."

He shook his head. "Glad I'm a VIP."

"Oh," Mackenzie said quietly, "I meant to tell you you're non-VIP. It's not personal. It's functional."

"VIP is a state of mind," he whispered.

She stifled a laugh.

"Today we're focusing on the basics," the teacher said. She walked over to a speaker and pressed a button. Accordion-heavy music started playing. "The posture, steps, and emotion fuel the beautiful connection between partners in tango."

"You're not a VIP," Mackenzie said quietly, keeping her eyes straight ahead.

"What am I, then?"

She glanced at him. He had a half smile on his face.

Her heart flew into her throat again. She looked away. "An honored guest, just like the rest of them, but your dinner will be served in the tent."

"Line up so you can see yourselves," the teacher said, snapping her fingers. She placed a hand on her trim stomach and stepped forward. "We are going to step slow, slow, quick quick, slow."

The room filled with the sound of shuffling feet. Mackenzie instinctively put her hands up, focusing on her reflection.

"Gentleman, you step *forward* with your left foot. Ladies, you will start back with your right foot." She demonstrated, then walked around the room, correcting them.

"Do you think I should add in some hip sway?" Cameron jutted out his leg.

Mackenzie snorted a laugh. "I don't think it's necessary."

"Good, very good!" the teacher said. "Now turn to your partner and try together. As they say, it takes two to tango!" She threw her head back and let out a cackling laugh.

Mackenzie bit her lip. Cameron was already facing her, holding out a hand. "Are you ready?"

"Yes. Always."

Mackenzie stepped forward, placing one hand in his, the other on his shoulder. His shirt was soft and warm.

Thankfully, her hand wasn't sweaty. Not yet.

A gentle touch fluttered to her side and landed on her hip.

"Slow, slow..." he muttered, looking down at their feet.

Mackenzie kept her gaze up. She relaxed her shoulders, leaning into the music, only being thrown out of it when he stepped on her foot.

"Hey," she said, "watch it."

Cameron laughed. "I didn't know you were so good at tango."

"It's my first time!" she said, beaming. "I guess I'm just good at everything."

He sighed. "I guess you are."

He raised his arm, sending her into a spin, and she twirled, laughing, her mind circling.

The song stopped. She stepped away, her chest heaving with breath.

"I didn't expect to like this so much," he said.

She smiled at him. "Tango?"

"Dancing with you."

The air let out of her lungs. "Ah."

"You're all doing wonderful," the teacher said. "Let's take a break. Please have some water and catch your breath."

Mackenzie was the first to the water cooler. It glugged and bubbled as she filled a paper cup with cold water. She walked to her purse and pulled out her phone.

"I'm sorry," Cameron said, low and near her ear. "Was that too forward?"

Mackenzie cleared her throat. "I wouldn't say that, but I have a policy."

"What?" He grinned. "You don't date salesmen?"

"I don't date salesmen I work with."

He nodded. "I see. Well then, that is a predicament."

"Isn't it?" She raised an eyebrow and drained the water cup. She crumpled it, tossing it into the trash.

"I'm sorry, it's been so long since I've met someone so..."

Mackenzie couldn't resist. She cut him off. "So much better at sales than you?"

He laughed. "Yeah. That's it."

Silence hung between them. She stared at him, trying not to smile.

"It's been a while. I, uh..." He scratched the back of his neck. "I had a bad engagement."

She raised her eyebrows. "Oh."

"I fell in love quickly and proposed. Her family hated me, though."

As much as she wanted to crack a joke, she couldn't. She was too focused studying his every hesitation, every sigh.

"They broke us up," he said, shaking his head. "They threatened me."

"Threatened you?" She cocked her head to the side. That was too wild, and somehow worse than her breakup.

"It's true. They had some criminal connections, if you know what I mean."

"What? Like the mafia?"

A smile broke his face. "I know how this sounds, but sort of. Yes. They ran me out of the country."

There were three voicemails waiting on her phone. Two of the numbers she recognized; one she didn't. Another call lit up her screen.

Why couldn't they give her a break right now?

"That's awful, Cameron. I'm so sorry."

"It's okay." He looked up at her, his eyes shining. "It's just to say – I'm not trying to rush anything with you, Mackenzie. I'm not trying to do anything. I just...like you. I can't help it."

She grinned. "Oh. I don't blame you."

He laughed. Her phone rang again.

"I'm sorry, I need to take this. I've got people trying to reach me at all hours and—"

"And you're getting threats from neighbors." He smiled. "I understand. It was nice to spend some time with you."

Her breath hung in her throat. "You too."

"I'll see you next Saturday?"

She smiled, stooping to pick up her purse. "Yeah. Saturday."

# Twenty-four

In the days leading up to the ball, Mackenzie's speed grew like a hurricane. Liam knew he shouldn't stare but, at the same time, he couldn't look away.

By the Monday before the ball, she was in a state, arriving for their meeting at the tea shop a half hour late, her hair atop her head in a bun with pieces shooting out, a pair of thick glasses squared on her face.

"Morning," she said, sitting down with a huff. "Sorry I'm late."

"Not a problem," he said. "I brought a coffee for you. I wasn't sure if Eliza would kick me out for it, so I've been hiding it under the table."

Her eyes widened. "You're an angel. I won't tell if you won't."

"It's cold now," he said, pulling the paper cup from under his chair. "But I think—"

She accepted it, her fingers brushing his hand. "It's perfect. Thank you."

He sucked in a breath. The plan he'd set for himself was slipping away faster than the morning fog. He wanted to speak up, but how?

That was the one thing he should've planned – an opener. Something to direct the conversation.

*We need to talk* seemed too serious.

*I have to tell you how much I adore and admire you* sounded like someone out of a bad movie.

*You make me feel like love is possible and there is still good in the world* didn't roll off the tongue like he thought it would when he'd come up with it at three AM.

He kept having this dream of Mackenzie running down the hill on the island, her shadow outlined with moonlight. She ran, always away from him, and when she reached the water, she was gone.

He woke half delirious, his muscles rigid. Liam made up his mind then and there that he had to tell her how he felt. He couldn't go on like this.

But looking at her now...it seemed like the wrong time.

He pulled a stack of flyers from his bag and set them on the table. "I picked these up. If you're happy with them, I can go to the post office and have the first batch mailed."

She picked up one of the flyers, flipping it back to front. "This looks great. Did you get any help designing this?"

Liam shook his head. "Other than some inspiration I found online, no."

"It looks awesome. I can pay you for your work. It's technically part of the project at this point."

He put up a hand. "Please, save it for Lottie. It was no trouble."

She took a gulp of coffee and squinted at the sheet through her glasses. Shadows of makeup hung beneath her eyelashes, with bits of black dusting the freckles on her cheeks.

What if he reached across the table and brushed them away? That was one way to start a conversation.

"You added a QR code, too?"

Liam sat back. Enough wild thoughts. "With a link to Lottie's website, yes."

"This is *so* helpful. Thank you, Liam." She set the sheet down. "I owe you something. Was there anyone you really wanted to meet at the ball? We don't have Granny's favorite coming, but if there's someone else, I could introduce you. Maybe someone in film?"

"At the ball?" He cocked his head. "I didn't think I was invited."

Her eyebrows scrunched together. "Of course you're invited! Why is everyone I like surprised to be invited while strangers make demands whenever they see me?"

"Do you need me to film something?"

"No, you're not – I'm not going to make you work. You're one of Lottie's friends, even if she doesn't know it yet. You have to come."

He grinned. "I'd like that very much."

"There will be some filmmakers there. I'm sure—"

"No." He shook his head. "It would be a waste."

She cocked her head to the side. "Why? You're making a film right now. It's what you went to school for. Isn't this your thing?"

He sighed and picked at the corner of his paper coffee cup. "It was, once. Not anymore. I've got a folder full of films no one will ever see."

For the first time, she smiled, her eyes wide. "You do? I want to watch them."

He shook his head. "No, you don't."

"I do." She picked up her coffee, the smile still reaching her eyes. "Why are you being so dramatic? Is this your artistic side?"

"No." Liam laughed. "I'm being dramatic because in film school, I used all of my savings to make a micro budget film with my friend and classmate."

"Yes," she said slowly, "you told me about that."

"What I didn't tell you was how that friend ran off with the film, took all the credit, and used it to launch his career."

He looked down, studying the doilies on the table. Elegant curves and intricate stitching. Maybe he'd underestimated the décor.

Mackenzie cleared her throat. "What I'm hearing is that it was a really good film."

Liam sighed. "Yeah, I suppose it was."

"Which means you're good at this!" She slammed her cup onto the table and he jumped. "Sorry," she said. "You can't give up so easily, Liam."

He shrugged. "Actually, I can."

"At least let me see the films you've made. Then I'll leave you alone."

"I'll send you the link."

She grinned. "Do you have something to wear? To the ball?"

He let out a breath. *Finally out of that line of questioning.* "Er, not really."

"That's okay." She stood, stuffing a flyer into her back pocket. "Joey is flying out to get a tux fitting. He can take you with him."

"Brilliant, thank you."

"I have to run, but thank you again for handling the flyer!"

He watched her disappear through the door. "My pleasure."

. . .

The next day, he and Joey flew to a tuxedo rental shop on the mainland.

"Even Eliza is feeling the pressure," Joey said, stepping out from behind a blue velvet curtain in a white tuxedo jacket and black pants. "Once it got out Bailey Jo will be there, the frenzy started all over again. People are hanging around the tea shop to plead for invitations."

Liam glanced over at him. "Did you get the OK to wear a white tuxedo? I didn't know that was an option."

A smile spread across his face. "I don't know that it is. What's Mackenzie going to do, turn me away?"

"Yeah, well," Liam turned back to the mirror. "She might."

"I look cool, though."

"You look like a waiter."

Joey laughed. "I kind of do, don't I?"

The last time Liam had worn a tuxedo was for his sister's wedding. It didn't feel much different this time around. The electric excitement in the air. The furrowed eyebrows over details. Copious amounts of cake.

Though, last time, it had ended with his sister sobbing into his shoulder. The woman he'd rented the tuxedo from made him pay an extra cleaning fee.

Joey made a face. "I think these sleeves are too short. I feel like a penguin." He flapped his arms up and down.

"If you do that all night, you should be able to hide that it doesn't fit," Liam said.

A sales associate stepped up to Joey. "Can I help you find a better size?"

Joey slammed his arms down to his sides. "Didn't see you there. Yes, that'd be great."

"Perhaps go for a bright orange this time?" Liam suggested.

Joey turned toward the sales floor. "Only if you do a complementing sky blue!"

Liam chuckled and shook his head. He wasn't interested in making a statement, unless it was to Mackenzie specifically. After she'd skewered him about not pursuing his film career, he was even more unsure how to proceed.

The sales associate returned. "How does it fit?"

"Very well, I think."

"I agree." She smiled. "Do you want to try anything else?"

He shook his head. "No, thank you."

How silly was he, standing here and looking at himself?

"I'll take this one, please."

She nodded. "Wonderful. I'll meet you at the front whenever you're ready."

He pulled open the blue curtain to his dressing room and stepped inside. There was a small mirror there. He stared at himself.

Perhaps he was nothing more than a coward. It had been so long since he'd talked about the film school incident. No one cared to hear his sob story, and he didn't care to tell it.

When he said it out loud, it didn't sound as bad as it had been. Or maybe he hadn't explained it well. It wasn't just that it had ruined his faith in his friend or his own future career. It ruined his trust in himself. He had poor judgment. How could he do anything if the one person he'd trusted had run off with their work to enrich himself?

Liam unbuttoned the jacket and replaced it on its hanger. Was he really foolish enough to believe Mackenzie was any different? She'd had many opportunities to behave unethically, and yet she carried on, doing what needed to be done.

Was she real? And how had he found himself on this far-flung island with her?

How could he not tell her how unbelievably lucky he was to have met her?

Liam walked it to the front of the shop. Perhaps the tuxedo could serve a different purpose this time. It could allow him to be someone else for the night – someone with courage.

# Twenty-five

T he days at the cottage melted away. Addy spent her time gossiping with Eliza at the tea shop, combing the coast at low tide for mussels and anemones, and running errands with Patty.

That woman was a tonic. She even made grocery shopping fun, and she always managed to pull Addy's thoughts away from the heavy reminders of her divorce.

"Endings are always messy," Patty told her. "No matter which way they go. It's best not to dwell. Pick up and keep moving."

"What if I don't know where to go?" Addy asked.

"Then jump in the water and move your limbs. You'll end up somewhere," she said with a nod. "You know how to swim, don't you?"

"Well yes, but – "

"Then swim!" she barked. "And, when you can, lay on your back and float. Don't miss the clouds and the stars."

It felt like a season for floating. Addy had no idea where to take herself, and the excitement around her carried her from day to day. The ball arrived in a flash, and along with it, more guests to the island.

AMELIA ADDLER

On Friday evening, the youngest Dennet sisters—Emma and Shelby—caught the last ferry in. After they arrived, they immediately went to the kitchen to snack on sugar cookies and bicker with Mackenzie and Eliza.

Patty and Addy sat at the table, watching Derby the golden retriever weave between legs to pick up crumbs.

"It's cool that the ball will have some celebrities," Emma said. "But why is everyone so *old?*"

Mackenzie glared at her. "Everyone isn't old. You're just young. Get it straight."

Eliza laughed. "I wouldn't cross Mack right now. She will defend this party to the end."

"Using her fists," Shelby added, waving a closed hand in front of her nose.

"It's not just a party," Mackenzie said, sighing. "It's a fundraiser for an important cause. Plus, it'll show Russell why he needs to pay me more."

"You're getting *paid* for this?" Shelby asked.

"Of course." Mackenzie scoffed. "Do you think I'd work for free?"

She frowned. "I assumed it was like an unpaid internship."

"An internship for what?" Mackenzie said.

"For being a concierge to rich people?" Emma suggested.

Addy stifled a laugh. If only her daughter had been able to make it to the island for the party. She would've loved to join in on teasing her cousin.

Eliza crossed her arms. "Mackenzie, would you say there's anyone else you want to impress with a super successful party?"

Mackenzie snapped her head toward her with narrowed eyes. "No. Why?"

Patty let out a cackling laugh, keeping her head down. She was carefully hand-writing name cards, even though Mackenzie had told her she didn't have to.

Mackenzie turned to look at her. "What's so funny?"

"I haven't gotten this much use out of my calligraphy pen in years," Patty said. "Look, I've just done Liam's name. Isn't that nice?"

"Very nice, thank you," Mackenzie said. "But he's not a VIP. He doesn't need a name card."

Patty shrugged. "He's VIP to me."

Derby, flattened out on the floor, scratched his nails against the kitchen tile, reaching for something under the cupboard.

"Ah!" Mackenzie yelled. "Who dropped an entire cookie on the floor? Derby almost got it!"

The girls erupted into laughter and started a mad dash to get to the cookie before the dog.

Addy leaned into Patty's ear. "What was that about?"

A smile crossed her face. She set Liam's name card in the center of the table. "Just a theory I have. I'll let you know after it pans out."

Before long, Mackenzie chased them off to bed to prepare for the day ahead, and the next morning, Joey flew to Seattle to pick up Sheila and Russell.

Addy was so excited to see Sheila she could hardly contain herself. She forced Patty to let her help with breakfast as they waited for them to arrive – much to Patty's dislike.

"I said I can do it myself!"

"I know you can," Addy said, pulling out a tray of warm bread from the oven. "But I won't let you."

They reached for the butter knife at the same moment the door in the kitchen flew open.

"Adelaide!" Sheila yelled, raising her arms.

Addy released the butter knife and it clattered to the floor. "Sheila!"

Her sister wrapped her in a tight embrace.

"We've missed you!" Addy said.

"I've missed *you!* I'm so sorry I wasn't here when you got to the island."

Addy laughed. "Don't be. I've had Patty, and you got to go to Europe with your boyfriend. How was it?"

Sheila sucked in a breath. "Really, *truly* spectacular. We're going back after the ball. Come with me! We can take a road trip to Italy."

"Ha! In my dreams, maybe."

"It doesn't have to stay a dream, Addy," Sheila said. "You don't have to worry about Shane complaining about how long the flight is or how small the hotel room is."

It was true Shane didn't share her love of Italy. She'd double majored in Italian and German. He'd thought even a vacation to Europe was nothing but a distraction.

"Just you complaining about how the taxi driver is dangerous?" Addy said with a smile.

"Welcome home!" Patty waved a rag. "I hope you're hungry."

"Always." She smiled. "Has Patty been nice?"

"I'm always nice!" Patty barked over her shoulder.

Addy grinned. It had been so long since she'd seen her sister. Too long. "She is. Everyone is nice. You've made a paradise here."

"Good. Maybe I can convince you to stay."

"Yeah, sure," Addy said. "Right after I do a tour of Italy."

"I'm serious," Sheila said, prodding her. "We need someone smart around here, Professor."

"Former professor," Addy corrected. "I was fired."

Sheila scrunched her nose. "Laid off, really."

The girls ran in, one after the other, hugging Sheila and pelting her with questions.

"Do they really say 'action' when they start a scene?"

"Did you eat Liège waffles for breakfast every day?"

"Did you get mad seeing Russell kiss Eloise Knight again and again?"

Sheila threw her head back, laughing. "Not at all. It's the magic of the movies! Eloise is a doll, too."

Addy sighed. "I can't believe you got to hang out with Eloise Knight. She can't be as charming as she seems in interviews."

"She is." Sheila nodded. "I could learn a thing or two."

"Who's Eloise Knight?" Emma asked.

"An old actress from Mom's era," Shelby said with a smile.

Sheila *tsk*ed. "She's not an old actress. She's a year younger than I am, which, actually..." Her voice trailed off, her forehead creasing with a frown.

"Best not to think about it," Addy said.

Mackenzie's footsteps thundered down the stairs. "Hey, Mom!"

"Mackenzie! How's my hero, leading the charge at home?"

She rolled her eyes. "Things are eerily calm right now. I haven't gotten any panicked calls or notices that the food spoiled or people have gone missing or the chairs caught on fire."

Shelby frowned. "Chairs on fire. Has that been a primary concern?"

"*Everything* is a primary concern," Eliza said with a slight smile.

Granny shuffled over with a large glass pan of casserole in her hands. "Eat up, ladies. This is my famous sausage, grits, and egg casserole. I don't want to hear any grousing about having to fit into your dresses later."

The complaints rolled in, but the casserole turned out to be —predictably—irresistible. They ate quickly, cleaned up, and then Sheila suggested a stroll by Cattle Point Lighthouse. She said it would be helpful to calm Mackenzie's nerves.

"I'm worried about her," Sheila said as they walked along the shore. Seagulls dipped into the water and, in the distance, sea lions lounged on rocks, their barks echoing. "Russell left her a lot of responsibility. She just had her heart broken, and you know Mackenzie. She can't say no to a challenge."

"She's had some help." Granny smiled, continuing down the narrow path that cut through the tall grasses.

Addy looked ahead. The lighthouse's whitewashed walls stood against the dome of blue sky. All around them, the ocean sparkled, a mosaic of blue and green.

"What's that smile?" Sheila asked. "What does that mean?"

"Her heart may not remain broken for long," Granny said, turning around and tapping her finger to her nose.

"Why are you speaking in riddles?" Sheila asked with a laugh. "Are you going to tell me what's going on or not?"

Addy shook her head. "She always speaks in riddles. It's like talking to the Island Yoda."

Patty threw her head back, laughing. "I like to have my mysteries too, you know."

She powered past them toward the lighthouse, the steep cliffs dropping off at her side.

"Don't worry about it," Sheila said. "I'll get it out of Eliza tonight." Sheila stopped, grasping Addy's hand. "I'm so glad you're here! How have you been?"

Addy shrugged. "You know. Good."

Sheila stared at her. "I mean really. How are you?"

It was too beautiful a place to be sad.

Yet here she was. "I've been better," she said.

Sheila squeezed her hand tighter. "Maybe you need to consider staying here a while. I don't know why, and I don't know how, but there might be answers for you here, too. *Someone* here for you."

Addy let out a laugh. "Yeah, that'll be the day. You didn't tell me there was magic for middle aged women on this island."

Sheila hooked her arm in hers. "It doesn't just look magical. There is a sort of magic to this place."

The breathless gasps of someone running built behind them. Mackenzie stopped short, her cheeks red.

"I'm only getting more nervous with all this walking around. We need to go home and get ready." She sighed. "Now!"

Sheila laughed. "You heard the woman. Everyone back to the car!"

# Twenty-six

I t was lucky Russell had offered his house for them to get ready. Even grabbing their things at Granny's cottage was a cramped mad dash.

"One of my shoes is missing!" Emma yelled.

"Shelby! That's *my* mascara!"

"I was just going to carry it over for you," Shelby hissed.

Mackenzie already had her go-bag packed and her dress hanging on the grab handle in her car.

She didn't have time for arguments. She needed to be ready for anything, because she knew everything was going to fall apart. She just didn't know when.

At Russell's house, the guys knew to keep out of the way – for the most part. Joey sat on the couch, fielding calls from party guests arriving at various nearby airports. Russell walked around with a silver tray filled with champagne flutes.

He stopped next to Mackenzie, seated at the kitchen island, a black towel draped over his forearm. "Champagne for the lady?"

Mackenzie glanced at him. "Why am I the only one worried about this ball? It was *your* idea."

"I hire the best so I don't have to worry," he said with a shrug.

"Don't try to flatter me, Westwood." Bubbles fizzed up the glass. "You left me a huge mess and went to Europe to party."

"I know." He frowned and picked up a glass. "Hey, did you know your mom had this champagne in a café in Paris? She loved it so much I bought a case, just for this occasion."

Mackenzie snatched the glass from him. "Now you're using my mom's happiness against me?"

She took a sip. Either his story had gotten to her or this was the best glass of champagne she'd ever had.

"Not against you, Mackenzie. Never *against* you. With you. To buoy you." He set down the tray. "I didn't expect things to get this bad. I'm happy to compensate you for your extra time and emotional distress."

She sighed, setting the empty glass back on his tray. "I'm not after money, Russell."

"Oh. What are you after?"

Mackenzie narrowed her eyes. "Everything. I want *everything.*"

A laugh sputtered out of him. "Oh. I'll see what I can do."

Eliza swooped in, grabbing a glass of champagne. "Just tell her she's the best and she'll be happy."

Russell turned to her. "You're quite literally the best, Mackenzie. You've single-handedly saved this operation over and over."

"Thank you." Mackenzie scrunched her nose, but couldn't hide her smile. "I'm going to expect a glowing reference for my next position."

"Done!"

Sheila walked in, carrying a Tiffany-blue box in her arms. "Big surprise, everyone!"

Granny sat in a chair at the dining room table. She turned to look over her shoulder. "Surprise, surprise. You were supposed to finish curling my hair."

"It's curled," Sheila said, dropping the box on the table. "I've got the hairspray here."

A few spritzes, then she opened the box. "When I was abroad, I bought a finishing touch for everyone to add to their outfits. No pressure if you don't like yours, but I couldn't resist."

She reached into the box and pulled out a pink and white floral crown.

"This is for you, Patty. I know you love flowers in your hair, and I saw it at the market in Waterloo and..."

Granny clapped her hands together. "Put it on! Put it on!"

Sheila delicately balanced it on her head, pinning it into place. She handed Granny a mirror. "What do you think?"

"I think I'm going to be the belle of the ball."

The room erupted into laughter. She stood up and kissed Sheila on the cheek, leaving an imprint of red lipstick. "Thank you. I love it."

"You're welcome."

"Me next, Mom!" Emma stepped forward. Her skin was an unnaturally even shade, layered with thick foundation. Her eyebrows were painted on dark, but her eyes were yet to be touched, making them look comically small. "What'd you get me?"

"I know your dress has rose gold accents, so I got you something to match." She pulled a rose gold bangle from the box. It was open, with tear drops on both ends. The pink gold caught in the light.

Emma slipped it up her arm, stopping above her elbow. "I *love* it! Thank you, Mom!"

She managed to kiss her cheek before Shelby hip-butted her out of the way. "Me next."

Sheila reached into the box, grinning. "These are chandelier earrings they let me keep from the movie."

Shelby shrieked, grabbing them. "I *love* them! Thank you!"

"Eliza?"

"I don't need anything, Mom."

She smiled. "I know you don't *need* anything, but I found an Edwardian-era ring that reminded me of you."

The black velvet box popped open. Inside was a silver ring with a clear, oval-cut sparkling stone surrounded by intricate filigree.

Eliza gasped, slipping it on. "Mom! It's so pretty!"

Joey appeared over her shoulder. "That is pretty."

"Do you like it?" Eliza asked, holding her hand to his face. "I feel like a queen."

"Is that a diamond?" Joey asked, scratching the back of his head.

Sheila shook her head. "No. I had moissanite fitted into it."

"Eliza would *never* want a diamond ring," Mackenzie said, biting her lip and staring him down.

Joey's eyes darted between them. "She wouldn't?"

Eliza patted him on the shoulder. "No, dear. You know I don't like impractical things."

"Ah, right." He frowned. "Impractical."

Mackenzie thought it'd be fun to get ready with everyone, but she could hardly sit in her seat. Her leg was numb from jiggling.

She stood up. "Mom, I appreciate you're really good at giving gifts, but I need to get going and I can't—"

Sheila held up a finger, then placed a purple bag in Mackenzie's hand. "This one is for you, sweetie."

Mackenzie sighed and pulled the drawstrings open. She tipped the bag over and out toppled a silver comb covered in delicate silver and white flowers. Each petal was its own wisp of silver, pearls dotted throughout.

"That's gorgeous."

"I thought you might like to have a little something."

She smiled. "I love it. Thank you."

Shelby trotted over. "I can get it to stay in your hair. Just give me five minutes."

She smiled. "Sure, fine. Then I'm gone."

True to her word, Shelby attached the little comb in Mackenzie's hair using a web of clear hair ties and silver pins.

Mackenzie looked in the mirror, turning her head and staring. "This is so classy. We need to send you to Europe more often, Mom."

"I agree." She laughed and kissed her on the cheek. "Okay, my beautiful girl. We'll see you at the ball!"

"See you all there on your *best* behavior!" she said, walking out the door. "And remember—none of you are VIPs, so stay in the tent."

"But we're VIPs in your heart, right?" Eliza asked, looking up with wide eyes.

Mackenzie waved a hand. "Yeah, sure."

. . .

Three hours until the guests arrived. Mackenzie bumped up the rocky driveway to Saltwater Cove, her dress hanging in the backseat of her car, her eyes scanning for danger.

Something was bound to catch fire. Or the barn could fall down. Her hands buzzed and tingled. *Something* disastrous was going to happen.

She parked near the house and got out of the car. Birds chirped, and the sun peeked out from behind a rolling white cloud.

Far too peaceful.

"Why, hello there!" Margie said. This time she wore a flowing white dress and a wide-brimmed straw hat.

"Hi, Margie. How are things?"

"Things?" She put her hands on her hips. "Things are great. How are *you?*"

Mackenzie slammed the door to her car shut. "I'm a little on edge, to be honest."

A smile spread across Margie's face. "Like a bride on her wedding day. Don't fear, Mackenzie! We're all professionals here."

"I'm not doubting you, I just—"

"No offense taken." She waved a hand. "Come with me. I will ease your fears, one by one."

Mackenzie followed her, feeling very much like a toddler on a tour at a museum.

They started at the barn. Golden painted chairs stood at the ready, the tables draped in white linens. Bursts of pink roses and white hydrangeas dotted vases throughout.

"How did you get hydrangeas?" Mackenzie asked.

"I've got connections," Margie said with a smile.

Bistro lights cast a warm glow on the enormous hanging banners of Lottie's past, present, and future.

"I added a painting of her cute little face, too," Margie said, motioning to a large canvas showing Lottie with her head above water, popping her tongue out. "I thought we could do a raffle for it and raise a little more money."

"That's a great idea," Mackenzie said, shaking her head. "I should've thought of it."

Margie laughed. "You're going to need to learn to let go a little, Mackenzie. There's nothing wrong with leaning on your friends."

She forced a smile. "You might be right."

Margie was on top of everything – the food would be ready early. The band was already set up. The red carpet was staged and secured. Little cookies shaped like orcas were ready to be handed out as people left the party.

Everything was perfect.

"Why don't you go inside," Margie said, leading her to the house, "have a cup of tea, and get yourself ready?"

"Do you mind?"

"Not at all."

Mackenzie fetched her dress and, inside the house, Chief Hank led her to an empty bedroom.

"I was told to prepare a cup of tea for you," he said. "A hot toddy, perhaps? To help you relax?"

Mackenzie snorted a laugh. "Margie helped me relax, thanks."

Her sisters had already done her hair and makeup. All she had to do was squeeze into her dress. She unzipped the garment bag and stared at it.

Perhaps she'd gone too bold with this, the floor-length gown in stunning red satin, a plunging neckline and ruffles at the shoulder.

When she'd initially rented it, it seemed like it'd be fun. Something glamorous for perhaps the only glamorous event she'd ever attend.

Looking at it now, however, she might've rented her way into looking like a gift bag stuffed with tissue paper.

She sighed. If her dress was the biggest disaster of the night, she'd be thankful. She wrestled her way into it and zipped up the side, then slipped out the door and back to the kitchen.

"Please don't make fun of me, I can't –"

A man stood in the kitchen in a sleek black tuxedo. He turned slightly, the light catching his chiseled features.

She stopped, her mind casting itself high to low. Who was this guy? One of Russell's movie star friends, crashing the party? How did he get in the house, and why was he so early?

"Mackenzie." Liam bowed his head slightly. "You look stunning."

"Liam." Her breath hitched in her chest. It had to be the dress. It was too tight. "You got a haircut."

He let out a small laugh, looking down. "Yeah, well. Anything for Lottie."

"You look nice." She cleared her throat, her heart pounding in her chest. "I thought you were..."

"Sorry. Was I not supposed to be here? I'd just finished helping Margie with a painting."

"What painting?"

"She'd asked if I could donate a painting of Lottie and –"

"You made that?" She knew her mouth was hanging open, but she couldn't shut it. "It's beautiful."

He scrunched his nose. "I don't think I did her justice."

"You did."

"Margie convinced me to set up an easel on the cove, too. She said the starlight on the beach makes for very pretty scenes." He paused. "Maybe you'll have a moment this evening to meet me there?"

Those eyes of his, full of warmth and mischief. The cut of his jacket emphasized his broad shoulders. His neatly trimmed hair stood slightly tousled, and his lips, always on the verge of a smile.

"Starlight Beach. I'd love to." She cleared her throat. Her head felt ready to pop. She needed to sit down. "Excuse me, sorry."

She turned, walking back to the bedroom and shutting the door.

Why was Liam so helpful? Making a beautiful painting of Lottie like that. Doing the fliers. Showing up early.

And since when was he so...*handsome?*

Mackenzie stood with her back against the door, taking deep breaths. She'd known there was a disaster coming to this ball. She hadn't known it would be her.

# Twenty-seven

Was it something he'd said? Liam went after her, but stopped himself when the front door flew open.

"Hank!"

Margie looked at Liam and stopped. "Hello, Liam dear. Have you seen my husband?"

He cleared his throat. "I believe he's getting dressed."

"I'm going to have to tell him to put his sheriff uniform on. The party crashers are already here!" She threw her hands up. "Ridiculous!"

"I'm happy to help if Hank needs a hand."

"Oh, do you mind? I swear, every time I turned around, there was a rustling in the bushes."

"Did you see someone?"

"No!" She dropped into a kitchen chair. "But I know they're there. It's like chasing chipmunks."

Hank walked in dressed in a navy blue suit. "We've got chipmunk problems?"

"Party crashers," Liam said. "I can scare them off. I just need to check on Mackenzie first. She seemed a bit frazzled."

"She did." Margie dropped her voice low. "I'm afraid that might not improve until the night is done."

"It has to," Liam said. "It's her big night."

He walked down the hallway and knocked on the only door that was closed. "Mackenzie? Are you all right?"

"I'm fine! Yes!"

He frowned, opening his mouth, but she spoke again.

"Is everything all right with you?"

"Erm, yeah. No problems here. Margie thinks there might be some people trying to sneak in. I'm going to go out and scare them off – unless you need anything?"

A clanking of the doorknob and Mackenzie appeared, light pouring in from behind her. "People are *sneaking in?*"

His breath caught in his chest. Soft waves of hair touched her bare shoulders. Her lips were red and full, her eyes sparkling, darting.

It was rude to stare, even at beauty. He looked away. "Don't worry. I'm sure it's nothing the Chief Deputy Sheriff can't handle."

"And you, apparently."

Liam laughed and looked up, his eyes meeting hers. "I'll see what I can do. Is there anything else you need before I go?"

Mackenzie opened her mouth. For the briefest of moments, he thought she was going to lean in and kiss him.

For the briefest of moments, his heart soared.

"No." She cleared her throat. "I don't know how to thank you. For everything."

One kiss and he'd call it even. "It's no trouble. I'm happy to help."

She smiled, a pained sort of parting of her lips, the lift not reaching her eyes.

If there was ever a time to be bold...

He cleared his throat and leaned forward. "The thing is, I don't know anyone at this ball."

"You know my granny."

He laughed a staccato laugh, his heart banging against the walls of his chest. "Right, Granny. But I was thinking, as much as I'd love to parade your granny around the entire night –"

Mackenzie laughed, covering her mouth with her hand.

He went on. "I'd also love to spend some time with you. One dance, at least?"

"Hm." She raised a finger to her chin. "That's easy enough."

"Great." He grinned and turned, stopping to add, "Try not to worry. It's going to be wonderful."

"You can't know that."

"I do." He paused. "Because you've done it, and I would trust you with my life."

She smiled. "Thanks, Liam."

Enough. If he kept going, he'd spill all his secrets, and he'd promised himself he would save it for a better time. "I'll see you later."

Back in the kitchen, Margie peered through the window and Hank finished the knot in his tie.

"I just saw someone go in the barn," Margie whispered. "Can you imagine the nerve of these people!"

"I can." Hank placed a hand on her shoulder and kissed her on the cheek. "Ready, Liam?"

His mind was firmly elsewhere. "Uh – yes."

"Here are the guest lists," Margie said, handing them each a tablet. "If you see anyone sneaking around and they're not on the list, they're out!" She clapped her hands together.

Hank turned to Liam, eyebrows raised. "She means we take them on the boat and throw them overboard."

She *tsk*ed. "I did not say that."

Liam hid his smile.

"Let's go, kid." Hank walked to the front door and opened it.

Liam followed. "I thought suits weren't allowed at black-tie events?"

Hank shrugged. "I'm wearing what I've got and I've got what I'm wearing."

If only Liam could be so bold. Maybe he would've kissed Mackenzie right there, at the house. What was the point of waiting? Was it really for her benefit? Or to satisfy his own fear?

They walked outside, into the sun, and spotted the first party crasher wandering inside the barn.

She was a middle-aged lady in a sequined, knee-length purple dress with a feather protruding a foot above her gray hair.

"Can I help you?" Hank asked.

"I'm here for the party. Ball. The party-ball." She flashed a smile, pink lipstick on her teeth.

Hank crossed his arms over his chest. "Are you sure about that? I have a list here, and if your name's not on it, I get to take you down to the county jail for trespassing."

A scowl twisted her smile.

The woman slammed her hands to her sides. "Fine. I'll go willingly. But I'm not happy about it."

"I'll make sure you find your way." He nodded to Liam. "Let me know who else you find lurking around."

"Sure."

Liam branched out, walking the perimeter of the property. He talked to the band, asking if they'd seen anyone.

"I swear I heard a boat come up to the shore."

Liam shut his eyes. "You've got to be kidding me."

He walked down to the cove, stepping carefully to avoid getting sand on his shiny shoes.

Sure enough, a couple dressed in their finest sat on the wicker chairs he'd helped Margie set up, green beer bottles in their hands.

Time to channel his inner Hank. "Can I help you?"

The man glanced up at him. "We're good, thanks."

It was probably his own fault for sounding more like an eager shopkeeper and less like the authoritative town sheriff, but still. Annoying.

"I'll need to check your names against our guest list," Liam said, pulling out the tablet. "The party doesn't start for –"

"I said we're good," the man snapped before turning to his date and forcing a laugh.

Liam narrowed his eyes. There was something familiar about him. Something about his tone...

"You're that whiny boat bro, aren't you?" Liam said. "I remember you. Crying about not getting your way at the dock."

He stood. "Yeah, well, that video really blew it out of proportion."

"And I'll blow *you* out of proportion if you don't get out of here."

He didn't even know what that meant, but it sounded like something Hank would say, and it felt right.

The guy glared. A drop of sweat streamed from his temple and dropped off his chin. The woman sat back, tapping on her phone.

Liam stepped forward. "Call whatever boat dropped you off and have them pick you up. Now."

Boat Bro flinched, reaching for his phone. "Fine." He made the call. "Didn't want to be here anyway."

Within seconds, a rubber dinghy hummed toward them.

"It was worth a shot," the driver said as he pulled the boat onto the shore.

The couple climbed in. Liam waved. "Have a nice evening. Look out for sharks."

The woman's mouth dropped open. "Are there really sharks?"

"No." The bro bumped into her, forcing her to move from her seat. "Probably not."

Liam stood on the shore, grinning. "Au revoir!"

Spurred by his success, Liam walked the property for the next hour with Hank. They didn't find anyone else and soon moved to stand at the entrance of the red carpet.

"I know there are some celebrities coming," Hank said, staring down at the tablet. "But I couldn't recognize them if you paid me a hundred bucks a pop, so maybe you can help with that?"

Liam wouldn't notice them either, but for a different reason. There was only one woman on his mind...

"Sure," he said.

"According to Margie, they're starred on the list."

Liam searched the names on his phone, finding pictures of the VIPs.

"I know that one," Hank said, pointing at a picture of Bailey Jo. "Her songs are catchy."

A laugh burst out of Liam. "I wouldn't have taken you for a Bailey Jo fan."

"I'm a complex man, Liam." He crossed his arms over his chest and nodded a hello to a woman with a camera. "Morgan! Nice to see you."

She stepped toward them. "Hey!"

"She's doing the pictures tonight," Hank said. "Best photographer on the island."

She rolled her eyes. "Yeah, yeah."

"Where's Luke?" Hank asked.

"He's doing a video for tonight, setting up a shot of the trolleys coming in."

Liam would have to find Luke. Footage from the ball might add something to the documentary.

He waved a hello to Morgan, and she offered a handshake.

"Look alive," Hank said. "We've got our first takers."

A red trolley pulled up and stopped at the bottom of the hill. A steady stream of people spilled out of the front and back doors, a never-ending line of laughter, voices, and yelling.

Liam got to work immediately, confirming names. Two women swooped in to help. Hank said they were Margie's daughters.

They survived the first wave, then caught their breath as Morgan snapped pictures of the partygoers.

"Are these prints for sale?" Hank yelled. "I need a new headshot."

"No," Morgan barked. "Get back to work."

Another trolley, another twenty minutes of chaos. The guests were, at least, in good spirits. All smiles and easy laughs, and not even the VIPs were offended when Hank asked their names.

The party was underway, music carrying on the wind, the smell of fried onions and roasted chicken wafting over.

"You can go," Hank said to Liam. "Enjoy yourself. I've got one of my deputies coming to help cover soon. Shouldn't be many more arrivals."

A trolley pulled in at that moment with a ding. "I'll stay for this one."

It stopped and people poured out, this trolley somehow was even more full than the last.

Liam was busy checking off names when a face caught his eye.

He looked up, squinting. It couldn't be. He waved a group through, not checking any names, instead searching, staring.

It *was* him. Cameron Walters. His stomach turned to stone.

"No. No. You're not coming in here." Liam said, walking toward him and waving a hand.

Cameron's eyes brightened, a smirk on his face. "Liam, please. Don't embarrass yourself."

Liam stepped closer, his face inches away. "I don't know what your game is here," he said, his low voice dragging over stones, "but whatever it is, you're not doing it."

He smiled and put a hand on Liam's shoulder. "Check the list, old boy."

What choice did he have? He clenched his jaw and searched for Cameron's name.

He spotted it and looked up.

Cameron clapped him on the back and massaged his shoulder. "Thanks so much. Enjoy your night as an usher."

Liam pushed his hand off. "I need to go."

"Go on. Have a good time," Hank said, not looking up from his tablet.

He had to talk to Mackenzie. Liam spun, slipping through the trees and onto the path to the house.

# Twenty-eight

J ust what he needed – Liam Yorkley pushing his way back in.

"Hang on." Cameron turned his head and smiled. "This is my good side."

The woman with the camera snapped a picture. "Thanks."

He tried to blink the flash out of his eyes. She was quite good-looking. "Will I be seeing you at the party later?"

Her eyes were focused on the camera lens. "No."

"That's a shame. We could've gotten to know each other a bit better."

She looked up, eyebrow raised. "Do you mind? You're in the way."

He turned. Behind him, at the bottom of the red carpet, a black SUV sat with its door open. Bailey Jo stepped out, her long leg peeking out of the slit of a lilac gown.

"Bailey Jo!" He smiled, rushing to greet her.

"Hi, Cam," she smiled, gathering her gown with her hands and walking past him.

Flashes erupted around her, not just from the photographer, but from the cell phones of guests on the red carpet.

Whatever. He could catch up with Bailey Jo later. He had more pressing issues. He needed to talk to Mackenzie, and not just about Liam.

Cameron had made up his mind. It would be best for everyone if she worked beneath him, or maybe as his sidekick – handling people like Bailey Jo while he dealt with the business side of things.

She could start right away. Maybe Bailey Jo would have more famous friends here? Russell was sure to have friends. Mackenzie could start unofficially working for Opuluxe tonight, striking while the iron was hot.

He cut through the red carpet and into the crowd.

Where could she be? He peered around the band. Couples bumped into him as they danced.

He walked through the open doors of the barn, brushing shoulders with people standing in the way.

Not there either.

He walked back out and spotted her standing under the massive white tent.

Cameron smiled and walked toward her. A red dress clung to her curves. She looked good.

She would look better on his arm.

"Mackenzie!" he called out, waving.

She turned, her eyes setting on him, and she smiled. "Hello there."

"You clean up nicely."

"Can't say the same for you," she said, lips pursed.

"Ha. Sorry I was late."

"There's no such thing as late to these sorts of things," Mackenzie said. "I'm glad you made it."

"Me too." He paused. "I had some trouble getting past your bouncers."

She scrunched her eyebrows. "We don't have bouncers."

He looked around. No sign of Liam. That was lucky. He'd gotten to her first.

Mackenzie's grandma was there, glaring at him. What had he done to offend her? There wasn't time to care.

He put his arm around her, walking her away from the eavesdropping group. "Do you remember when I told you about my engagement? The family threatening me?"

"Yes."

He leaned in, close. "I can't believe this, but one of them is here. My ex-brother-in-law – whatever you want to call him. He must be stalking me."

Mackenzie shut her eyes. "You're kidding. That's terrible."

"I know." He sighed, stepping in front of her. "It really creeped me out."

"Who is it?" Mackenzie's scanned the crowd. "I can have Chief Hank arrest him."

"That's not necessary. I'm just surprised he's here." He took both of her hands in his. "His name is Liam." He paused. Her eyes didn't move. "Liam Yorkley."

Mackenzie bit her lip. "Liam? Are you sure?"

"How could I forget?" He laughed. "I thought I'd have to flee to the American embassy to get out of the UK safely." He laughed. "Kidding. Kind of."

She looked over her shoulder, then back at him. "Liam's harmless."

Cameron narrowed his eyes. "What makes you think that? His family is dangerous. They're smugglers."

"I thought they did boat tours."

"What do you think is *really* on those boats?" He sighed. "Hopefully your interactions with him haven't been as dangerous as mine. Do you know him?"

She opened her mouth and sucked in a breath. "I do."

"Do you...like him?"

"He's Russell's artist in residence. He's been involved with Lottie."

"Involved?"

She laughed. "Yes, involved. Why do I feel like I'm being interrogated?"

He put his hands up. "I'm just trying to make sure you didn't fall into his clutches."

She pulled her hands away. "I'm generally against falling into clutches."

He put his hand on her waist and pulled her close. "Well, good. I wouldn't want anything to happen to you."

She stared at him, her mouth slightly open.

It was better if she didn't keep asking questions. He wasn't about to lose her connections because of Liam showing up.

He applied gentle pressure, leading her to the dance floor. "How about that dance you promised me?"

# Twenty-nine

H e pulled her away from her mom, her sisters, Reggie and Granny, right in the middle of Granny's story about haggling prices with a shopkeeper when she lived in Poland.

Mackenzie stopped. "I might need to go back to –"

Cameron cut her off. "Come on. One song. It sounds like a good one."

Why was he being so pushy?

She looked over her shoulder. Every member of her family looked away at the same time.

They weren't going to rescue her.

Maybe she could make an excuse? That she needed to check on the food, or powder her wig, or count the seashells on the seashore?

"Is your mom going to sing tonight?" Cameron asked, moving her once again.

They reached the dance floor. They needed to start moving. Otherwise, they'd be in the way.

She put one hand in his, and the other on his shoulder. "No."

He stepped forward, stomping on her foot.

Mackenzie gritted her teeth. "I didn't know we were going to salsa."

"Sorry," he said, looking down. "Let's start over."

He pulled her back and stepped left, then right. This time she was able to follow.

"I'm impressed with this setup," he said. "You should know you have a knack for it. A way with people."

"Thanks."

"Are you at least going to get Bailey Jo to sing?"

"No way," she said. "I think she wanted to avoid having to perform."

By *I think* she meant *I know.* This wasn't a karaoke bar. She wasn't going to drag people onstage to perform for free.

"You have to make her!" He threw his head back and laughed. "I'm sure she'll be a good sport about it."

"It doesn't seem fair," Mackenzie said slowly, looking down at her feet. Her toe throbbed.

"Just tell her it's for charity." Cameron grinned. "For the fish."

She looked up at him. "You mean Lottie?"

Cameron threw his arm out, sending her into a twirl. One, two, three times around.

Her head spun. She stopped. "Lottie is a whale. Whales aren't fish. They're mammals."

"Yeah, I know. It was a joke."

He spun her again one, two times. She broke free of his hand.

"The smuggler thing. Was that a joke too?" she asked.

"About Liam?" He grabbed her hand again. "No. That was true. If I were you, I wouldn't mention it to him."

"Why not?"

He sighed. "Criminals don't like being called out."

*Criminals.* Her stomach lurched. "I think I need to get something to eat."

She stepped backward, away from him.

"Are you okay?" he asked.

"I'm just a little dizzy. I'm fine," she said.

He put his arm around her shoulder. "Let me get you something."

His touch felt heavy, dragging her down. She wriggled out. "I just need a second."

The song ended. She made her escape through the barn's open doors just as Russell's voice boomed over the microphone.

"Hey everyone! I don't want to spoil the fun, but I wanted to thank all of you for coming out to support Lottie. We've had our share of setbacks, but I'm confident that, with our amazing team, we can get through anything. I'd like to thank Sheila, of course. You kicked it all off. Our contractors..."

Silence, that was what she needed. She'd lock herself in a bathroom – if she could get to it.

A wall of bodies had formed at the entrance of the barn.

"Excuse me," Mackenzie whispered, trying to push through. She could still feel Cameron's touch on her skin, burning, grabbing, pulling. Was he chasing her? She didn't dare look back.

It was like he was all over her suddenly. He hadn't been like that when they'd danced the other night.

Maybe that was what changed. She'd opened the door to something romantic and he turned into an eight-armed octopus.

"And, of course, a huge thanks to my assistant Mackenzie Dennet. She stepped in at the last minute and rescued all of this."

*Oh no.*

She stopped and spun around, a smile frozen on her face. "Thank you!" she mouthed with a nod.

"You're not getting out of it that easily," Russell said with a laugh. "Get up here."

The bodies around her parted, and a path opened to the stage.

Oh, *now* they'd get out of her way?

She drew up her shoulders and walked, the smile frozen on her face until she reached the stage and accepted the mic from Russell.

"Hi, everyone." She stared out. The sun was setting now, the sky getting its first hints of yellow and orange. She licked her lips, scanning the crowd, looking for her mom or Eliza or Granny.

One face stood out. Liam. He leaned against the side of the tent, his expression flat.

Her heart skipped a beat. She cleared her throat. "It's been an honor to be a part of this project. I will be hitting all of you up for more donations in the coming weeks."

Laughter rippled throughout the crowd. She looked back at Liam. He stared, arms crossed.

"This project is the culmination of thousands of man hours, people from all walks of life working together to right a wrong from decades ago." She was getting too philosophical. She sucked in a shaky breath. "Enjoy the food, enjoy the music, and enjoy the night!"

She passed off the microphone and stumbled off the side of the stage, falling to her knees. The drummer jumped to help her back up. She thanked him before rushing off.

Where was Liam?

Cameron had to be confused. Liam wasn't frightening. His family couldn't be criminals.

Though he did brag about bribing officials in South America...

Mackenzie wasn't afraid of asking him what was going on. But what would he have to say for himself?

# Thirty

The sky opened in front of him, shots of pink and red across a yellowing sky. Liam sat in a wicker chair, staring at the flames of the fire, his shoes dusted with sand.

The water was calm and the music was dampened, as though he'd filled his ears with cotton. His brain was muffled, too, ideas and sounds bouncing without landing.

He let out a sigh.

"Liam."

He glanced up. The moon shined like a beacon over her. "Mackenzie."

"I'm sorry I didn't get to check in with you sooner," she said, walking closer. "Is everything okay?"

He returned to the flames. "I think so, yes."

"Are you having fun?"

He looked up, locking onto her eyes. "How do you know Cameron?"

She took a seat next to him. "Cameron Walters?"

He blinked. "How do you know him?"

She sat back and shrugged. "He was working with Bailey Jo and offered me a job as a saleswoman."

Liam scoffed. "Is that what you were doing with him back there? Negotiating terms of employment?"

"I'm sorry," she snapped. "Was I supposed to ask your permission first?"

"Don't be coy with me, Mackenzie."

"I'm not being coy. He told me about you."

"About me?" Liam stood, first walking away from the fire, then turning back. "Did he have nice things to say?"

"Not really," Mackenzie said. She bit her lip. "He said you were dangerous."

A laugh burst out of him. "*I'm* dangerous? And you believed him?"

She sighed, pushing herself off the chair and standing, the red gown dancing off her curves like an impossible painting. "He said he was engaged to your sister."

"That's true." Liam scanned her eyes. Her lips. There was no sign of what she was thinking. "Did he tell you how it ended?"

She looked back at him. "Did you threaten him, Liam?"

"What?" He rolled his eyes. "Of course I did. He left her at the altar."

She looked down, away. Something sparkled in her hair, throwing dazzling flashes every time she moved. "Why did he leave her at the altar?"

"I don't know. Because he's an animal. Because he was trying to use her and use our family."

"Your family? Why?"

He sighed. "If you're so close with him, why don't you ask him? Ask him about his last business opportunity."

"I'm asking you." Her tongue grazed her lips and she sighed. "Your family...are they involved in anything illegal?"

"I don't know what you mean."

He narrowed his eyes. What could Cameron possibly have been on about? The worst his family had had to deal with was drunken passengers.

"Do you know about a time they've smuggled anything?" she asked.

The fire crackled, a branch collapsing into a pile of hot ash, floating up in a plume.

He stared at her, the heat of the flames on his face. "No."

"He told me"—she cleared her throat—"that your family are smugglers."

He looked up, past her, into the orange sun. "And you believed him."

"I don't know what to believe, Liam! Why don't you give me your side of the story?"

"There's no story, Mackenzie." He snapped his head back at her. "Everything I told you was the truth. My parents operate boating tours for tourists." Above him, the cloudless sky hung dark blue. "My sister had a terrible, botched engagement to a man who used her and left her. I didn't think to mention it to you because I didn't think in my wildest dreams he'd show up here."

Mackenzie clasped her hands together. The corner of her mouth flinched.

"And I didn't think," he added, lowering his voice, "you'd be foolish enough to trust him."

"I can't read your mind, Liam. How was I supposed to know –"

"You were supposed to *think*, Mackenzie!" His voice boomed in the small cove, bouncing off the rocks and trees and chairs. "I never thought you, of all people, would be blinded by a smooth-talking salesman and a high-paying job."

"I need a job, you know. Not everyone can travel the world painting hillsides."

"Is that what he was offering you? A job? Because it looked like he was interested in something else. You have no idea what you're getting into."

Her face contorted, her nose and forehead scrunched. "Spare me, Liam. I can take care of myself."

He could take the hint. She'd clearly made up her mind.

"Then I wish you all the best."

He brushed past her and into the night.

# Thirty-one

H er chest burned. It was the fire, burning too hot for too long.

Mackenzie walked away from the flames and toward the water. The brilliant sunset she'd been waiting for was rapidly disappearing. Waves lapped quietly on the shallow shore, and the dark sea met the last wisps of light blue sky. Above her, darkness grew like an inescapable dome.

Her ribs strained against her dress. It was too tight, and her lungs were overstuffed with air. She forced herself to release a breath. In, out, as shallow as the waves.

Who did Liam think he was? He probably *was* a criminal, skating by on good looks and a charming accent. Had he even denied his family being smugglers?

She couldn't remember. All she could see were the flames dancing in his eyes, the curl of his lip.

"Oh, sorry," a woman's voice said.

Mackenzie spun, her eyes landing on Bailey Jo. She'd come to the ball in a simple black dress, her hair cascading down her shoulders in glamorous curls.

"It's no problem," Mackenzie said. "I was just leaving."

A smile lit her face. "Mackenzie, right? You work for Cameron?"

She clenched her jaw. She'd almost forgotten Cameron existed. "I don't, no."

"Oh." A frown creased Bailey Jo's face. "I must have made a mistake. He said you..." Her voice trailed off and she narrowed her eyes.

She stepped forward. "He said I what?"

If he'd told Bailey Jo she was a smuggler, too, that might be part of a pattern.

"I'm not sure."

Mackenzie smiled. "I don't work for him. He's trying to get me to work for him, though."

"Ah." She scratched the back of her head. "He wants me to recommend him to my friends."

"Sounds like him."

"But I told him *you* were the one who came up with my trip."

Mackenzie smiled. Beamed, really. "Yes, well, I did."

"He said you work for him, and he was great with planning. Like..." She bit her lip. "Planning this ball, which I'm starting to realize might've been a stretch."

Mackenzie's eyes could have popped out of their sockets. "Cameron said he planned *my* ball? He was barely invited!"

"I don't want to start anything." Bailey Jo smoothed her dress with her hands and floated down, landing in a chair.

She was much smaller in person. She looked like a little girl to Mackenzie, though she was only a few years younger.

Bailey Jo went on, shaking her head. "He's been calling me nonstop. I had to block two of his numbers. I had no idea he'd be here, too – I'm hiding while my ride pulls around."

Mackenzie groaned. This might be worse than him making up a lie about her being a smuggler. She put a hand to her face and rubbed her forehead. "You're kidding. So he's a pest."

Bailey Jo leaned forward. "I..." Her voice trailed off. "I'm glad you don't work for him."

"I don't, and I'm going to ask him to leave immediately."

"Please don't," Bailey Jo held up a hand. "I don't want to cause trouble. It doesn't take much to be called 'difficult' as a woman, you know."

"Oh, believe me, as a difficult woman, I know." Mackenzie laughed. "It's not just you. He's caused other problems."

The smolder in her chest faded, now a molten lump in her stomach. Cameron flashed through her mind, his hands pulling at her waist. He was always pulling. Always taking.

Mackenzie shuddered and shook her head. "I think he may be wanted by an international crime family. Or Scotland Yard. I'm not sure."

Bailey Jo laughed. "Good to know I'm not the only one he's bothered."

"No." Mackenzie threw a glance over her shoulder. Stars shone above, as if someone had poured them into the clear liquid sky.

"It really is beautiful here," Bailey Jo said.

Mackenzie took in a breath. "It is."

"I think I'd like to get a place on the island. Somewhere I can get away."

"Do it! I was on the fence about moving here, but it's been worth it."

Mackenzie's eyelids fluttered, too many scenes flashing in her mind. Liam on the dock. Liam laughing over a cup of tea. Liam's dark, brooding scowl lit and shadowed by the flames, the snap of her accusations sitting in his eyes.

He was the one who'd made it worth it.

Tears flooded her eyes. She bit her lip.

"Maybe you could help me if I move?" Bailey Jo said. "I'd like to be able to enjoy the islands without getting swamped with people." She paused, then rushed to add, "Not that I don't appreciate my fans."

"I get it." Mackenzie put a hand on hers. "You know, you remind me of my little sisters."

Bailey Jo raised her eyebrows. "Is that a good thing?"

"Yeah. I like them. A lot. And I always want to help them, so I'd be happy to help you."

Bailey Jo clapped her hands together, laughing. "Yay!"

"If you throw on a wide-brimmed hat and some sunglasses, you can hike here and no one will give you a second glance."

Bailey Jo grinned. "That sounds wonderful."

"I'll give you my number, then I'm going to go kick Cameron out of this party. It's long overdue."

"Good luck!"

. . .

The food didn't run out, the band didn't stop playing, and every bag of goodbye cookies found a loving home. They managed to replenish the money Russell's old assistant had stolen, plus a few thousand extra. By all measures, the ball was a success.

Mackenzie asked Chief to find Cameron and remove him from the party. He obliged, no questions asked. She watched as he walked him out.

Bailey Jo stayed until the end, joining Mackenzie and her fangirl sisters on the dance floor. She even requested a picture with Mackenzie, which she promptly posted online with a call for donations, resulting in another fifty thousand dollars from her fans alone.

The next morning, Mackenzie sat in the tea shop, the muscles in her back stiff from a dance move gone wrong, her head throbbing. There was a price to pay for fun, and Mackenzie had accrued interest.

A cup of fermented tea sat next to her phone on the table. She took a deep breath and picked up the cup. Would it be rude to wear sunglasses inside?

A call from Cameron lit up her screen and she stared at it. On his second attempt, she answered.

"Hello." She picked up the tea and held it near her nose. It smelled of vinegar.

"Mackenzie! I just saw Bailey Jo's picture! Are you two besties now or what?"

"You might say that." She set the teacup down. It tasted like vinegar, too, stinging her tongue. What was Eliza thinking? This tea was awful. They shouldn't be selling this poison.

"I'm sorry I had to cut out early. We had an emergency and I had to fly out."

"Wow," she said, her voice flat. The cup clattered on the saucer as she pushed it away. "Crazy you could leave in the middle of the party you planned. What if something went wrong? How would we have reached you?"

"Ha, Mackenzie, listen..."

"No." She cut him off. "You listen, Cameron. If you ever take credit for my work again –"

He interrupted, his voice silky smooth. "Mackenzie, I didn't take credit for it. I hope I'm not preemptive in saying this, but I like to think of us as a team. Almost like...a power couple."

Bile hit the back of her throat, burning. Was it the tea, or was it because Cameron used her ex's favorite phrase? The one he'd deployed to use her all those years?

"We're not a power couple." She drew herself up. "We're not any couple."

"I'm not trying to rush anything, Mackenzie. You know that."

"There's nothing to rush. Don't call. Don't write. If I ever see you on this island again, I'll have you arrested."

He scoffed. "You don't own the island."

"Try me."

Silence.

She went on. "And stop harassing Bailey Jo. You're embarrassing yourself."

Mackenzie ended the call and slammed her phone on the table. The teacup jumped.

Eliza stood, staring with wide eyes. "Who was that?"

"Nobody."

She wiped her hands on her apron and sat down. "Are you okay? Too much champagne last night?"

Mackenzie narrowed her eyes. "No."

"Ah." She smiled. "Then it must be a hangover from throwing a great charity ball."

Mackenzie grunted.

"Maybe you need to start planning the next one!"

"There's not going to be a next one, because Lottie isn't ever going to get here."

"Hey," Eliza said. "Don't snap at me. It's not my fault."

"You're right. It's mine." Mackenzie sunk into her seat.

Eliza's tone softened. "I didn't say that."

A jingle rang out and Joey walked through the door, a pair of aviators in his hand.

"Good morning." He pecked a kiss on the top of Eliza's head. "What's the special for today?"

"Apparently it's an extra grumpy Mackenzie," Eliza said with a smile.

Mackenzie glared at her. "I'm not extra grumpy. I'm realistically grumpy. The ball was a waste of everyone's time."

"I had fun," Joey said.

"It's not about you!" Mackenzie glared at him. "The vote is coming up and my stupid flyers aren't working."

"What flyers?"

Mackenzie reached into her purse and pulled out the glossy card with Lottie at the top. "This one. The one explaining how they're trying to make it illegal to transport Lottie here. Did you get one of these in the mail last week?"

He took it gingerly in his hand, flipping it back to front. "Was I supposed to read this?"

"Yes!" she shouted.

"I remember getting it, but I thought it was just about Lottie coming back."

Mackenzie shut her eyes. He was the fourth person to tell her that today. She'd asked all the regulars at the tea shop, plus all the cashiers at the grocery store that morning.

Not a single one of them had read it. One woman had told her, "I lump all the junk mail together to recycle. I don't even look at it."

"Joey isn't our target audience," Eliza said. "I'm sure people are reading it."

"I'm sure they're not." She stood, grabbing her purse off the floor. "Also, Eliza, I love you, but this tea is horrible and you should throw it out."

She bit her lip, smiling. "Is there anything else you want to tell me?"

"No." She turned toward the door.

A gentle hand touched her arm. "Hey," Eliza said. "What's going on?"

"Nothing." She put her purse on her shoulder. "I'll see you later."

Mackenzie stormed down the path to the cottage, the wind in her eyes. She wasn't fit to be in public.

So what if she could throw a fun party? The party didn't matter. The picture of her with Bailey Jo didn't matter, even if Steve ended up seeing it and feeling envious.

Mackenzie didn't care about that anymore. She should've been focused on what needed to be done to get Lottie here safely. Instead, she had been thinking about stuffed mushrooms and hydrangeas.

It was glaringly obvious, especially in this blinding morning sun—she was a fool.

Inside the cottage, she rushed upstairs and shut the door. She didn't want to talk to her mom, or Eliza, or even Granny.

The door popped open and she looked up. Derby stood with his mouth open, panting.

"Okay," she said softly. "I guess you can come in."

She sat on the bed and patted the blanket with her hand. "Come on."

He wagged his tail as he walked over, then braced himself for the small jump. His back legs froze, so Mackenzie bent to lug him onto the bed.

"You're not a puppy anymore, Derby."

He turned, whacking her with his tail, and flopped onto her lap.

She laughed. "I guess I'm staying here for a while."

Her laptop was within reach. She propped it on a pillow nearby, clicking through her email, then the news, then a whole lot of nothing.

She pulled up an email from Liam where he'd sent her a link to the movies he'd made. At the time, she had been too busy to watch them.

Or at least that was what she'd told herself.

She opened it and clicked on the first video. A small brown bird appeared on the screen, pecking at the ground. It picked up a dime, then took off, dropping it.

The dime rolled and the camera cut in close, past a sleeping dog, down a sidewalk, past a waiter dropping a tray of glasses, all the way down to a guy kneeling.

He looked up, love in his eyes, a ring in his hand.

A splatter of white hit him in the face.

Mackenzie laughed, covering her mouth. The little brown bird swooped in, taking the dime back.

How had Liam gotten it to look like the bird was doing that? What's more, how had he made an entire story, and made her laugh, in a two-minute film?

She didn't realize it at first, but tears spilled from her eyes, dropping from her cheeks and onto Derby's head.

What had she done? In all her fury, in her need to win and conquer, what had she lost?

# Thirty-two

There wasn't much to pack. Liam was used to living in small spaces – and leaving them.

A row of blank canvases leaned against the walls of his room. He'd give those away; he had artist friends he'd met at the farmer's market. Hopefully Cameron hadn't gotten to them, too.

All his paintings had sold except the one of Mackenzie in front of the tea shop. Maybe it made him soft, but he couldn't sell it, and he wouldn't leave it behind.

One day, he might hang it up somewhere, then close his eyes and remember the warm rays of her smile and the ocean breeze against his skin.

Maybe that would be enough.

It was small and when he pressed it against his shirts, it fit into his suitcase. The zipper strained as he closed it.

Liam stepped outside. The morning air was thick with dew and light danced on the water. There was no one around—not a contractor, not even Joey.

He pulled out his camera and set up a shot. A black bird floated on the surface, its belly puffed and splattered with drops of water. Tufts of yellow grass swayed in the wind, far off islands rising from the water like the mountains behind them.

A boat bumbled into the dock, and a man with a yellow tool-belt stepped off, shaking hands and laughing.

What was the point of this? Filmmaking had never brought anything good to him. It was all dashed hope and betrayals. Dark clouds and explosive words. Why even try?

He wasn't going to finish Lottie's documentary. Liam's first instinct had been right; he never should've agreed to try this. He'd give Russell the footage he had and release any claim to it. Surely someone else could finish the job.

Liam stopped the camera and zipped it back into its case. Maybe some dreams weren't meant to come true. They were meant to be given up and sold secondhand. Or maybe some dreams were never meant for *him*, even if they jumped from moving planes and every day with them felt like summer.

A white dot appeared in the sky and he squinted, tracking it with his eyes. The seaplane landed and Joey hopped out, tying it off.

"Afternoon," Liam said. "I've got something for you."

"Is it Tylenol?" He stood, sweat dotting his forehead. "Because I could use some."

Liam grinned. "No, sorry. It's a tuxedo. I was hoping you could return it for me."

"Oh, that." He laughed. "I was going to fly out there tomorrow. Do you want to come?"

Liam sucked in a breath. "I can't. I'm leaving."

"You need a ride? Where are you going?"

"No, but thank you." He stared out across the water. The waves were either playing a trick on him, or a small fin had just broken the surface. A porpoise, maybe?

"Will you be back in time for Lottie getting here?" Joey made a face, the corner of his mouth twisting down. "*If* she gets here."

Liam snapped his focus back to Joey. "What do you mean *if*?"

"Mackenzie is convinced the vote won't be in Lottie's favor. She told Eliza and me that people are just throwing the flyer away. Not even noticing it."

A fin broke the surface again, this time accompanied by a tiny spout of air.

Definitely a porpoise. They were incredibly shy. Liam hadn't gotten a chance to see one yet, and now for one to be so close to the dock? Remarkable.

"Yeah, well. That's a risk with mail, I suppose." Liam sighed. "I'm sure Mackenzie will find a solution."

Joey smiled, eyeing him. "Are you two having a fight?"

"No." He put his hands in his pockets. "Not so much a fight as she's convinced herself I'm a criminal."

A laugh burst out of Joey. "Really? She used to think I was a criminal, too."

Liam smiled to himself. "That's right. Joey the bank robber. She told me about that."

"Joey the bank robber," he repeated. "Yeah, that's Mackenzie. She's been touchy ever since her ex-boyfriend proposed to her coworker. Guess that would mess with your head."

"Jealousy can do strange things." Liam scanned the water. Would it pop up again? What would Lottie make of a little porpoise near her pen?

"Oh, sorry, I didn't explain that right. He proposed to someone else *while* they were together."

Liam turned to face him. "What?"

"She didn't tell you?" He puffed out a breath. "Whoops."

"I had no idea. When was this?"

"Just before she moved here," Joey said. "He convinced her they were going to get married and then *POW!* She found out he'd gotten engaged to someone else they worked with. Like she'd never existed."

Liam blinked. They'd talked about him, he was sure of it. But she'd left out that detail. "I can't believe she didn't tell me."

Joey raised his eyebrows. "Really? I mean, if you know Mackenzie, you know that's exactly the sort of thing she'd hide. I only found out because I was here as it was happening. She has a hard time trusting people."

Liam's phone dinged. **Your ferry to Seattle is on time. Please be sure to arrive thirty minutes before departure**.

It was leaving in three hours. What could he do in three hours? That wasn't even enough time to absorb what Joey had told him.

"Everything okay?" Joey tilted his head.

"Erm, yeah. I've got a bit of a timing problem."

Life was better when things moved slowly. The tide came in, steady and slow. The moon never rushed to wax and wane.

Liam didn't like to rush, but when he'd booked this ferry ticket last night, he was sure his time was up. As much as he'd admired what Mackenzie was doing, and how honest she was, she thought he was a villain. He wasn't going to convince her otherwise.

"Listen, man," Joey said, his voice low.

Liam was pulled out of his thoughts and nearly jumped. "Yeah?"

"I have to be honest with you," Joey continued. "Eliza sent me here."

"To do what?"

Joey tossed a look over his shoulder and leaned closer. "She told me to be subtle, but I don't think we have time for subtlety."

Liam laughed. "And you are terrible at being subtle."

"I mean, I think I do okay for myself," Joey said, waving a hand, "but whatever. She told me to tell you about the ex-boyfriend."

"Why?"

He sighed. "Because Mackenzie looks like she's giving up on Lottie and she won't tell Eliza anything and Eliza is convinced it's because of you."

Liam shook his head. "What have I got to do with it?"

"I don't know, man. Eliza sent me here and thought I could get you to talk to Mackenzie."

"I'm a criminal, remember? I don't matter."

He shrugged. "She wouldn't have come up with a theory about you if you didn't matter to her. She's making excuses to protect herself. Or, at least, that's what Eliza told me."

His heart leapt into his throat. "Right, well. I can't really do anything about that." He turned. "I'll go get the tux."

Joey sighed. "Stay in touch?"

"Sure."

He turned, walking back up to his room.

# Thirty-three

There were dozens of films on Liam's website. Mackenzie told herself she'd stop after one more, then another, and another. Some were shorter, two or three minutes. She watched those multiple times.

The longest was half an hour. It opened with a shot of a woman standing in a chapel, wearing a knee-length white gown, flowers hanging at her side.

"He should be here any minute." Her voice cracked. "Right?"

A stone sunk in Mackenzie's stomach. This was Liam's sister. She saw the resemblance immediately, and as much as she wanted to shut the laptop and walk away, it was impossible. Mackenzie sat there and watched, weeping all the way until the end.

"I suppose it's lucky, in a way," Liam's sister said, sitting with a cup of tea. "Some people go through a whole marriage before they find out the person they love is a git."

Liam's laughter burst out from behind the camera. Mackenzie jumped, sure for a moment he was in the room with her.

"So you've saved yourself some time, then?" he asked.

"I have." She looked to the side, her eyes searching. "He's the one missing out. All of it and, for him, all the time in the world won't help. I may look pathetic right now, being left behind, but it's him who's pathetic. He's the one who ran away. He'll always be the one who runs away."

The screen went black.

Tears dropped from Mackenzie's cheeks and onto Derby's head. He sighed, leaning into her, his eyes closed.

Mackenzie didn't want to be someone who ran away. She wanted to apologize, to tell Liam she'd been wrong.

But how could she? How could the word *sorry* encompass how sick she felt? Not just for believing Cameron over him, but for entirely missing who Liam was, every day not seeing the man in front of her?

She stood and dusted the fur off her lap. "Enough laying around," she announced.

Derby yawned, putting his head down, his round eyes peering up at her.

"Not you, Derby. I'm talking about myself."

The idea clapped into her mind all at once. It was like nothing she'd ever done before.

She pulled out her phone and took a deep breath. It was time to make a call.

"Hello?"

"Russell. It's Mackenzie. We need to talk."

"Sure. What's up?"

"Where are you?" She flew down the stairs and stuffed her feet into her shoes.

"I'm at home. Is everything okay?"

"I'll be there in two minutes!" She hung up, sprinting along the path to Russell's house.

The front door was unlocked, so she let herself in. Her mom sat at the kitchen island.

"Mackenzie!" She stood.

Mackenzie gave her a quick kiss. "Hey, Mom. Can't chat right now."

"Oh, okay."

"I found something, Russell. I mean – I discovered someone."

Russell cocked his head to the side. "Discovered?"

"Yes! Liam. Look!" She slammed her laptop onto the kitchen island and hit play.

It was the video with the dime. She watched their faces light up with frowns, then laughter.

"That's only one of them," Mackenzie said as soon as it was finished. "He's got tons. He's incredible."

"Not to be pedantic," Russell said. "But technically, I discovered him."

She sighed. "You saw Liam's films?"

"Yeah. Why do you think I asked him to make a documentary about Lottie? The guy's got talent."

She could scream. She thought they had spent all their time talking about wolves. She'd assumed Russell was, well, careless. "Why didn't you tell me about these?"

He put his hands up. "Another ball dropped. I'm sorry. Why does it matter?"

"He deserves recognition! He should have been discovered years ago."

"Well, I'd hoped the Lottie documentary would bring him some attention. If attention is what he wants."

"Of course it's what he wants! He's just horrendous at advocating for himself."

Russell smiled and looked at Sheila. "I know someone else like that."

Sheila scoffed. "Leave me out of this!"

"I don't think he's going to finish the Lottie documentary and it's my fault," Mackenzie said. "I can't explain. How do I get him noticed? Can we email this to one of your friends?"

Russell sighed. "You can, but it wouldn't help. His best bet would be to submit these to a few film festivals. Some of them are so short they'd probably waive the fee."

Mackenzie's eyes widened. "Film festivals? And he'd get discovered?"

"I think so, yes. He has a lot of talent and a history of telling exceptional stories."

She opened a blank document on her laptop. "Give me the top five. No – the top ten film festivals. I'm going to submit for him."

Russell grinned. "Sure."

# Thirty-four

Liam shut the door behind him, the echo bouncing off the empty walls. He didn't have time to deal with this. His ferry to Seattle was on the way. He'd already booked a hotel room. He'd solved this problem, and staying behind wasn't part of it.

He glanced at his watch and sighed. Staying meant seeing Mackenzie again. It meant watching Cameron run his hands on her back and spin her around. It meant having to hold his tongue.

His stomach lurched. He couldn't do it.

Bags. He needed to get his bags. One over the shoulder, one in hand. The tuxedo, zipped closed, draped on top. He dragged the canvases outside. Someone would pick them up. He'd figure it out later.

Down at the dock, Joey had disappeared. The seaplane floated on the water, looking too peaceful. Liam hooked the tuxedo hanger on the door. Hopefully the wind wouldn't blow it down. If it did? Oh well.

A sputtering engine announced the arrival of his ride. It was a small boat, not as convenient as the seaplane, but he didn't want to bother Joey...or have to answer any more questions.

It was a short, choppy ride to Friday Harbor. Water sprayed onto his face and sunglasses as Liam sat, staring ahead.

He unloaded at the dock, then sat on a bench until his ship arrived. The timing was perfect – not too much time sitting around waiting. Within an hour, he'd gotten in line and taken his seat at a window inside the express ferry.

Watching San Juan Island disappear over the horizon gave him a moment to breathe. He pulled out his laptop and put on his headphones. The thing he felt worst about was leaving without talking to Russell about Lottie's documentary. They'd never had a formal agreement but until last night, he'd planned on delivering *something*.

It was a waste, but what was he going to do? Liam opened the file with Lottie-related videos and clicked through. A shot of Lottie in her tank. Mackenzie fighting with Mrs. Smitt. Mackenzie fighting with the dock bros. Sea pen netting arriving on a cool and misty morning. Mackenzie flying in a plane...

Maybe he couldn't make a documentary. But maybe he could do something else.

Liam opened a new project and named it "Lottie," dropping videos in rapidly, sorting them, sketching out cuts in his mind. He was tangling with the wording of the opener when he felt a tap on his shoulder.

He jumped, pulling off his headphones.

"Sorry, sir," the woman said. "I just wanted you to know we've arrived in Seattle."

"Right. Thank you." He slammed his laptop shut and gathered his things.

It was easy to get a cab to the hotel with a view of the city he'd booked downtown. Normally he wouldn't book something so expensive, but he'd made so much selling paintings that he'd decided to splurge.

At the hotel, he dumped his things and got to work at a small desk by the window. Dinner that night was courtesy of room service. He stayed up until three, finally giving up when blinking failed to clear the soot from his eyes.

The rest of the week went on in this fashion. He made a little time to sightsee, stepping into Pike Place Market, walking along the streets. He went to a coffee shop to apply to some stopgap jobs, surprised when he heard back within a day.

It only took a week to throw something together. There wasn't anything he could do about Mackenzie, but at least he could do something for Lottie.

He sent it off into the world and bought a plane ticket. It was time to move on.

# Thirty-five

"Have you seen this?" Eliza asked.

Mackenzie looked up from her omelet. Granny had made it just the way she liked it – Gruyere cheese and sautéed mushrooms – but she'd only choked down one bite.

It'd been a week since food was appealing. She always felt full, and when she didn't, her stomach hurt. Either way, not much was getting in.

"I don't know what you're talking about," Mackenzie said, putting her fork down.

Eliza sat next to her, pushing the plate out of the way and setting down her laptop. "This video about Lottie."

Just what they needed. More trouble. Mackenzie shut her eyes. "What now?"

"No, it's a good thing! Watch."

A shining figure appeared on the black screen. It was Lottie, breaking the surface, blue water filling in around her. A spout of air puffed out and she rolled to her side, clicking and whistling. Text appeared on the screen.

*Lottie the whale was captured off the coast of Washington state 41 years ago. Actor Russell Westwood is leading the charge to bring her home.*

The scene cut to Russell sitting on his patio, the ocean at his back. "She's spent her entire life alone. Performing. Entertaining. It's time to give her a break. We're working with veterinarians, biologists, and an entire team of dedicated contractors to build Lottie what's essentially her own retirement community. It's been a wild ride."

A bird's eye view of the sea pen site flashed onto the screen – the buildings, the shoreline, birds dipping into the water. A harbor seal, plump and lazy, sitting on a rock. Piano music faded in as a time lapse ticked by, the sun rising and falling as boats buzzed in and out, the site coming alive.

Mackenzie pulled her arms in close. Goosebumps rippled on her skin.

Inge the whale researcher appeared, her eyes clear, her smile wide. "We have an incredible opportunity here. Lottie is a member of a close-knit family we've been studying for decades. We believe her mother is still alive and well."

Another woman appeared with the words *Lottie's Former Trainer*. "She could have a chance to live another forty years here. If she stays in that tank, by herself, I don't think she'll survive another five years."

A rollercoaster roared across the scene, and Lottie's tank dropped into view, centered under the midday sun. Paint peeled from the railings in flaking chunks. Lottie floated in the water, blowing bubbles. Stadium seats fanned behind her, a lavender pantsuit making its way down.

"How was I supposed to know Lottie was about to become the most popular whale in the world?" Mrs. Smitt barked.

Mackenzie gasped, spotting herself on screen. Sunglasses on her head, a stern look on her face. Was it possible? Did she look kind of...cool?

*Not everyone is happy to see Lottie move on.*

The screen froze on Mrs. Smitt's sour face, her lips pursed, her red lipstick smeared.

*Next month, Initiative Measure 81823, The Protect Marine Mammals in Washington Initiative, will go to vote. If it passes, moving Lottie will be illegal.*

An image of Lottie faded in, opening and closing her mouth as she squeaked. The view zoomed out, showing her alone in the tank, surrounded by barren walls.

*Vote NO on Initiative Measure 81823 and help bring Lottie home.*

Tears flushed Mackenzie's eyes and she bit her lip, trying to contain the hot breath coming up her throat.

Eliza turned, grinning. Her smile fell. "What's wrong? Why are you crying?"

"I'm not crying," Mackenzie said, wiping at her eyes. She let out a breath. The hot feeling in her throat passed. "It's just really good. Who made it?"

Eliza smiled. "Who do you think?"

"Liam?" Mackenzie turned back to the screen. "He hasn't answered my texts or my calls. Joey said he left the island. He's just...gone."

"But clearly not gone in spirit," Granny said, sitting down, a mug of tea in her hand.

Mackenzie cracked a smile. "Did you know about this, Granny?"

She blew on her tea. "Mm, not exactly. I knew I liked him. Not like that rude Cameron, who left me standing like a dope with his tea."

Eliza's phone rang and she snatched it to her ear. "Hello?"

Her eyes grew round and she cleared her throat. Mackenzie leaned in. Could it be Liam? Was he finally ready to talk to her again?

"Hello, Steve," Eliza said, rolling her eyes.

Mackenzie's mouth dropped open.

"Mackenzie's great." Eliza looked up, listening. "Uh huh. Sure. I'll let her know."

Eliza ended the call and set her phone down. "That was Steve, wondering why he can't get through to your phone. He was worried and wanted to make sure you're okay."

Granny let out a huff. "I bet he was worried!"

"I blocked him." Mackenzie covered her mouth with her hand. "I can't believe he's trying to pretend her cares about me all of a sudden."

"He can't stand to see you shine," Granny said, patting her hand. "Those types of men never can. They're invertebrates."

A snort came out of Eliza. "*Granny!*"

"What?" Granny looked around. "Is that a bad word now?"

"It doesn't even make sense!" Eliza said.

"It does. No spine. No backbone." Mackenzie smiled. "Speaking of invertebrates, I blocked Cameron, too."

Eliza clapped her on the shoulder. "Good for you. Seriously."

"That Steve," Granny said, wagging a finger. "I bet he saw you with Bailey Jo, running everything, and he wanted to take control of you again. Knock you down."

Mackenzie shuddered. "Never again."

"You can't give the time of day to a man like that." Granny took a sip of her tea. "Now Liam. There's someone you shouldn't lose track of."

"Yeah. I know." Mackenzie sighed.

Except she had no idea where he was, and he didn't want to speak to her. She'd never get a chance to thank him for the video. Never get a chance to tell him how sorry she was. Or even tell him about the two film festivals that had accepted his work. She'd have to email him and hope he opened the message.

Granny slammed her mug on the table. Eliza and Mackenzie jumped.

"If you agree with me," Granny said, "why aren't you out looking for him?"

Eliza tilted her head to the side. "Yeah, Mackenzie. I thought you had all kinds of tricks up your sleeve?"

She narrowed her eyes and opened her mouth. Nothing came out. Mackenzie stared at them. Neither budged.

She sighed. "Excuse me," Mackenzie said, getting up from the table.

• • •

It wasn't like she could just chase Liam down and force him to talk to her. That wasn't how it worked. She had no idea how it was supposed to work, but not like that.

Mackenzie flattened out on her bed.

"What does Granny know, anyway?" she muttered, flipping onto her back.

She winced, listening for footsteps on the staircase. Hopefully Granny hadn't heard that. It would end in a lecture, and Mackenzie didn't need a lecture. Saying it out loud sounded foolish enough. She knew she was wrong.

She let out a long breath. It seemed wrong to go after Liam, though. He'd clearly left for a reason, and that reason was her. Their fight, the nasty words they'd thrown back and forth.

He left the island without a peep. He wasn't looking to duke it out with her. Liam was above that.

And yet...he'd made the video. Mackenzie could tell herself it was just for Lottie, but then why did he include her in it?

Maybe it was Liam's way of saying goodbye. It seemed like something he would do – work on something quietly, in the shadows, not accepting any thanks for his brilliance. Then send it off into the world without telling anyone and without asking for credit.

It was a total Liam move, and Mackenzie was an expert in taking him for granted. She was an expert at living a life in the shadows, too, just as she'd done with Steve.

Mackenzie jolted upright, her breath quickening. Is this who she was? Someone who only felt comfortable dating in secret? Never choosing a partner in the clear light of day, some-one who was capable of kindness and gentleness and brilliance?

She had been so ready to believe Cameron was a nice guy and that Liam came from a family of criminals. Why was that? Was she really that intent on sabotaging any chance at real happiness?

*No.* She wasn't going to live like that.

Mackenzie got up.

It didn't matter if Liam didn't want her to go after him. She had to. She had no choice – unless she wanted to spend the rest of her life cowering in the shadows.

She fetched her laptop from the desk. There was work to be done.

# Thirty-six

Leave it to Liam to move to Hawaii during peak tourist season. Outside of his hut, there was an endless stream of couples holding hands on the beach, weddings at sunset, and family photo shoots.

It wasn't technically a hut, but it felt more adventurous to refer to it that way, not as a damp studio apartment with stained carpets and an army of cockroaches.

He'd applied to the job on a whim. Free housing and a low stress job as a zipline instructor? What could be better?

Liam was a fool – an overly sentimental fool who now grumbled at the sight of the mountains rising into the mist, the golden beaches, the overabundance of waterfalls, and the sparkling turquoise waters.

Every bit of paradise reminded him of her. Every serene scene reminded him Mackenzie wasn't here.

Liam lasted a week and a half. He walked into his boss's office at the end of the day and handed him the keys. "I'm sorry. I can't do this."

The kid peered up from his visor. "Did you forget to secure someone to the line?"

"No, nothing like that. I just have to go." Liam shrugged. "It's not personal. Actually, it's extremely personal."

He waved a hand. "Sure, whatever. I'll need you out of the room by the end of the week."

"I'll be gone."

Being alone in a beautiful place normally set him straight, but now, it felt like he'd never be righted again. Maybe it was time to go home. Do a full reset. Let his mum cook for him as she was always threatening to do.

"Hey," his boss called out. "Someone was looking for you."

Liam stopped. "Yeah?"

"I told them to wait on the beach, but there's a wedding, so I don't know where they went."

"What did they want?"

He shrugged. "I don't know."

"Who was it?"

He put his sunglasses back over his eyes and leaned back in his chair. "Not sure."

Liam gritted his teeth. "Thanks for that."

He walked out of the office and into the sand. Palm trees curved to the sea and cabanas stood as the only refuge from the sun.

The wedding was well underway, vows being exchanged. He took off his sandals, the sand burning his feet, and walked on.

"Liam!"

He turned, looking for the voice, scanning the groups huddled on towels.

When he saw her, the sand beneath him shifted.

Mackenzie pulled off her large black sunglasses, a straw hat sitting atop her head. "Hey!"

He put an arm up to wave at her. "Hi."

Mackenzie jogged over. "I can't believe I found you."

"*I* can't believe you found me." He stopped a few feet short of her. "I think I'm having heatstroke."

She laughed and reached into the bag on her shoulder. "Do you need some water?"

"No, but thank you."

He didn't want water. He wanted to put his arms around her. He wanted to pick her up and spin her around and yell, "You're here! You're here!"

She cocked her head to the side. "What's wrong?"

"Nothing. I – uh. You look great."

"Thanks." She smiled and looked down. "I saw your video. About Lottie."

"Oh. Did you like it?"

"Liam, it's incredible. I loved it. You're an amazing story-teller."

"Well, it's Lottie's story. Not mine." He stared at her. Were those freckles on her cheeks? As if she couldn't get any pret-tier...

She took a step forward. "No, I mean you put together incredible stories. I watched all your films, Liam. I'm sorry it took me so long. You're truly brilliant."

He flashed a brief half-smile. "That film was my last. It was for Lottie. I'm done with it all."

"Just for Lottie," she repeated, nodding. "That's going to make this awkward."

"What is?" Her eyes were so beautiful in the sunlight. There were hints of gold and green in the cool gray.

"I did something, and you have to promise not to be mad at me. At least think about what I did and know it came from a good place."

His heart thundered in his chest. He'd promise anything to her now. "All right."

"So, I watched your films and they were incredible. I thought you were short-changing yourself by not doing anything with them. I talked to Russell about getting you discovered –"

Liam laughed. "I don't think it's that simple."

"It isn't." Mackenzie smiled, rolling her eyes. "But he agreed. He thought you were insanely talented and that was why he hired you. He said the best way to get your name out there was to submit your work to film festivals."

"Yes, I'm sure it is." He softened his voice. She was trying. He appreciated that, and he didn't want the smile to leave her face. "Though I doubt they'll be clamoring for anything I've done."

"No?" She bit her lip and sucked in a breath. "Because *Dime* was accepted at Telluride and LA Film Fest."

His mouth popped open. "Are you joking?"

She shook her head, her hair flying back and forth. "No. I'm not. Are you angry?"

"Not angry. I might die of shock, but I'm not angry."

She grinned. "I thought this could be the start of something for you, Liam. It's a small gesture, but I wanted to find a way to repay you for all the help you gave me...and Lottie."

"That's quite a big gesture, in fact."

"Well..." She took a step closer. "Sometimes we need big gestures when 'I'm sorry' won't cut it. Or when we're not good at apologizing."

A smile danced on her lips.

"What do you have to apologize for?" he asked.

"For being the worst. For not seeing you when you were right in front of me. For ever believing a word that came out of Cameron's mouth."

Liam leaned in "So he's not your..."

"No. He's not anything."

He couldn't keep the smile off his face. "Does that mean you're single?"

Mackenzie laughed. "Single and jobless, yes. A real catch."

"You are a catch, Mackenzie." He let out a breath. "You inspired me. Everything I did for Lottie – it was because of you. Most people are only in it for themselves, but not you."

"I know. I'm nuts."

"Mad as a chair," he said, nodding.

She burst into laughter. "Please tell me there's a 'but.'"

He took both her hands in his. "I thought you were too good to be true. It took me a while to admit you were real. To admit I'm crazy about you."

"Good." She puffed out her cheeks. "Because I'd feel pretty silly coming all the way here, only to leave empty-handed."

"Empty-handed? Do you mean I can come back with you?"

"You have no choice. We have a lot of work left to do, and I need you to be stateside. Plus, you need to prepare. Telluride is in a few weeks, and I'm not going to push you one way or the other, but –"

"Would you mind being my date?" He squinted. "Unless you're busy."

She looked up for a moment and shrugged. "Sure. I guess I could fit that in."

He pulled her in, kissing her fiercely, the palm trees bowing above them.

# Epilogue

The night of the special election, Addy stayed up late with Sheila and the girls. The mood was jovial and full of bickering. Mackenzie was the most tense, though Addy could tell Sheila was on edge, too.

The results for Initiative Measure 81823 trickled in through the night. 87% of Washingtonians voted **NO**, and the news called it just before midnight.

Eliza and Mackenzie jumped, hugging and screaming. Addy caught Sheila's eye. She let out a breath, the color returning to her face.

The next morning, Addy slept in and woke to an email from her old boss at the university. Though she'd been laid off, he'd been hopeful he could advocate for a different position for her.

"It doesn't seem like it's in the cards this year," he said. "I am so sorry, Adelaide. Losing you is devastating to our community."

He was never an expressive man in person, and his words made her blush. She put her phone away until after breakfast, when one of Patty's omelets steadied her stomach enough to face it again.

He'd ended the email with a final offer. "A friend of mine was looking for a professional Italian translator for some short stories. I recommended you without hesitation. I expect he'll be reaching out shortly."

Addy read the line again and again, a smile spreading across her face. She'd always wanted to do more translation work, but there had never been time among her other responsibilities. Could she really be so lucky?

She made the short walk to the tea shop, the ocean sparkling in the morning sun. The air was getting cooler, and she paused to savor the crispness in the air.

When she pushed open the door to the tea shop, Macken-zie's voice boomed. She was on the phone, yelling at someone.

Addy slipped into a seat across from Sheila. "She's back on her warpath, eh?"

"Seems so." Sheila smiled. "I'm so proud of her."

"I am too."

Sheila pushed a plate of chocolate chip cookies across the table. "I have to go back to Belgium this week. Come with me. We'll have so much fun."

Addy picked up a cookie and took a bite. "I thought about it, but I've got another plan."

"Oh?" Sheila raised her eyebrows. "What's that?"

"I'm going to stay here for a bit. Spend time with the girls. And Patty."

A smile lit her face. "I was hoping you might say that."

"I might have some work coming in for translations and..." Addy sighed. "You were right. There is a magic in this place."

"The nerve of these people!" Mackenzie said, slamming her phone down.

Sheila and Addy turned to her.

"Sorry," Mackenzie muttered. "I'm going to have to go to the mainland. Mrs. Smitt is trying to slow down Lottie's release. Not this time, Smitt!"

Sheila broke first, erupting into laughter. Addy wasn't far behind.

"I have to talk to Liam," Mackenzie said, ignoring them as she breezed out the door.

"Adelaide, you'll have to keep an eye on Mackenzie for me," Sheila said."

Addy grinned. "No problem."

Eliza emerged from the kitchen, a pot of tea on her hands. Addy sat back. Maybe she'd get to spend some time with Patty today. They could take a trip to the farmer's market. Or, maybe, she'd go into town and visit the shops on her own.

She wasn't afraid of being alone anymore.

"Look smart, ladies!" Patty said, busting through the front door.

Her boyfriend Reggie followed behind, a basket of flowers in his arms.

"We're making bouquets for the senior living home. Clear a spot. Come on now," Patty barked, pushing her way in.

Not that there was such a thing as alone in this place.

Addy stood, a smile on her face. She leaned in and breathed in the fresh flowers. What a magnificent day.

# The Next Chapter

## Introduction to *Spotted at Lighthouse Bay*

**Guarded hearts are the hardest to open, and his is more guarded than most. But that won't stop her from trying...**

Adelaide Ashbourne used to have it all. But that was before she ended up divorced, jobless, and facing a deadly threat from one of her ex's enemies. All she wanted from San Juan Island was peace. Instead, she got a handsome new bodyguard with demons of his own.

Rick Hayle knows he can protect Addy, but figuring out how to guard his heart against his beautiful new charge is another matter entirely. If he's not careful, he'll end up doing something that could destroy them both – like falling in love.

With secrets, past wounds, and a shocking family betrayal working against them, can Addy and Rick find the courage to fight for their potential happily ever after? Or are they doomed to remain star-crossed forever?

*Spotted at Lighthouse Bay*, book four in the Spotted Cottage series, is a sweet, inspirational, contemporary romantic women's fiction novel that can be read as a standalone. Download today and get ready to fall for Rick and Addy.

# Reader's Newsletter

Sign up for my reader's newsletter and get Patty's recipe for perfect cucumber tea sandwich!

Visit: https://mailchi.mp/6ecd258dee9f/fq4uemmwmv to sign up and get a free copy!

# About the Author

Amelia Addler writes always sweet, always swoon-worthy romance stories and believes that everyone deserves their own happily ever after.

Her soulmate is a man who once spent five weeks driving her to work at 4AM after her car broke down (and he didn't complain, not even once). She is lucky enough to be married to that man and they live in Pittsburgh with their little yellow mutt. Visit her website at AmeliaAddler.com or drop her an email at amelia@AmeliaAddler.com.

# Also by Amelia...

## The Spotted Cottage Series
*The Spotted Cottage by the Sea*
*A Spot of Tea*
*A Spot at Starlight Beach*
*Spotted at Lighthouse Bay*

## The Westcott Bay Series
*Saltwater Cove*
*Saltwater Studios*
*Saltwater Secrets*
*Saltwater Crossing*
*Saltwater Falls*
*Saltwater Memories*
*Saltwater Promises*
*Christmas at Saltwater Cove*

## The Orcas Island Series
*Sunset Cove*
*Sunset Secrets*
*Sunset Tides*
*Sunset Weddings*
*Sunset Serenade*

Made in the USA
Coppell, TX
10 December 2024

42222744R00146